LYNNE WAITE CHAPMAN

MURDEROUS HEART
By Lynne Waite Chapman

Copyright 2018 by Lynne Waite Chapman
Published by Take Me Away Books
Cover design by Cynthia Hickey

This book is a work of fiction. Names, characters, places, and incidents are the product of the author's imagination and are used fictitiously. Any resemblance to actual events, locales, or persons, living or dead, is coincidental.

All rights reserved including the right to reproduce this book or portions thereof in any form whatsoever – except short passages for reviews – without express permission.

All rights reserved.

ISBN-13: 979-8-8690-7501-7

Chapter One

Ow. My lashes fluttered open, only to be met with a beam of light shooting through the window. Struck in both eyes. Not the way I wanted to wake up.

Well, good morning, sun. I pulled the pillow over my face and wiggled to the side of the bed before removing it to peek outside. Tree-tops swayed on the other side of my window. Another beautiful morning in small-town Indiana. My bed was warm and soft, and urged me to stay and watch birds flit from branch to branch for a while. Cooler temperatures had signaled leaves to begin their transformation from green to red and yellow.

I'd drifted back to sleep when the rapping on the door jerked me into reality.

Crap. What was wrong with people? Much too early for visitors.

It took a moment for my foggy mind to clear, and I remembered agreeing to this early morning visit. What had I been thinking? My friend Clair had arrived right on time. Having renewed her mission to get me into good physical condition, she'd set up yet another power-walk schedule.

I rolled out of bed and grabbed a sweatshirt from the chair to pull around my shoulders. After shuffling to the door, I pulled it open and gave Clair what I hoped was a dazzling smile. My ever-energetic friend jogged in place on the porch until I pulled the door open wide enough for her to jog in.

"Did I wake you?" The twinkle in her eye indicated she knew the answer and thought it was hilarious.

"No. I've been up forever."

In my dreams.

"Just haven't gotten around to making coffee. I'll load the coffee maker and get dressed."

Clair hopped around the living room in her imitation of a prize fighter. "You should try a bottle of water instead. It'll wake you up just as well and be healthier."

I stood at the kitchen counter pulling out the coffee canister. "Um. No. I have a cold or allergies or something. The caffeine will help clear my head." I loaded the pot and flipped the power button.

"Are you sick?" Clair stared at me, possibly in an attempt to see if I had spots.

"No, just a stuffy nose."

"Drink orange juice." She jogged over to the refrigerator, yanked open the door and stuck her head inside. "You don't have any. No juice at all. Well, you'll feel better after our walk this morning. It increases blood circulation and builds up resistance."

"Right." I didn't know if my friend was an expert on staying healthy, but I couldn't remember her ever being sick. Had to admire the woman for her boundless vitality and her spirit. She embraced regular exercise and was determined I would, too.

"You know, we're of that age." Clair and I had known each other all through high-school and she'd taken an interest in my well-being when I'd returned home after twenty-five years.

"Yes, I know we're in our forties and have to work harder to stay in shape." I'd heard the mantra before. According to Clair, all my body parts were destined to head downhill and reside somewhere around my ankles if I didn't become more active.

The pot made sizzling noises signaling coffee was brewing, so I wandered to the closet to find sweatpants and a reasonable matching shirt. Clair was fashionably dressed in black and yellow striped leggings with coordinating t-shirt and jacket. I didn't own anything to compete or even two pieces that matched. I was happy with clean.

She called from the kitchen. "Mason's dish is empty. Did you feed him already?"

"Um. No, I guess not."

Fortunately for the feline, Clair knew her way around my kitchen. The pantry door squeaked open and his dish rattled as it was filled with kibble.

I toted my shoes to the kitchen and grabbed a mug of coffee, taking it to my vintage walnut dining set. The sweet black and white kitty sat beside his dish and glared at me as I tied my shoe-laces. "You don't have to act like I starved you. I'm sorry I was a little slow with the cat-food this morning. I would have gotten around to it before I left."

I leaned back in my chair and savored the last dregs of coffee.

Clair, who hadn't let up dancing around the room, grabbed my empty cup and trotted to the sink with it. "Let's go, girlfriend. It's a glorious morning."

With a deep, fortifying breath, I followed her into the chilly morning air. As soon as she hit the concrete Clair set off at a fast walk. I jogged to catch up and settled into keeping pace, one step behind her.

My amazingly physically fit friend launched into her morning monologue. As usual she expected me to contribute. But even after being on the exercise routine for weeks, I wasn't able to participate in the rolling conversation while walking.

Clair didn't notice, or ignored, my lack of participation, and happily changed subjects at random. "I have an appointment to show a house at ten this morning. That gives us an hour and a half to walk before I have to get home to shower."

"How long? Hold on. Are you trying to kill me? I thought we were keeping it to forty-five minutes."

"Yeah, I know, but you should be ready to increase your time by now. You've been doing great. Stretch yourself. Reach for more!"

My cheerleader.

"Not today."

"Alright, how about sixty minutes?"

"Sixty? I could die in that amount of time. When I collapse you'll have to carry me home."

"Okay. Forty-five minutes. Just concentrate on your stride and don't worry about how long you're walking. I'll keep track of it and let you know when the time is up."

"Right" *I'd fallen for that pitch before.*

Clair pumped her arms and powered on. "What do you have planned for today?"

I spit out an answer. "I'll be writing. Have a couple articles I want to tweak before sending them in to the magazine. After that, laundry and scrubbing the house. Never gets cleaned while I'm in the middle of writing."

With my last puff of breath I concluded my side of the conversation.

Clair kept marching on, not even working up a sweat. She pointed out the trees and points of interest as we passed. "The storm the other day took down some limbs. Park service will have to get out here and clean up."

"The wind was hard on my trees, too. There are a lot of sticks in my yard that I'll have to pick up. My windows need washed." I threw in the part about the windows for Clair's benefit. I didn't plan to wash them. Not while I could still see out.

Clair slowed up to walk beside me. "I'll come over and help you with the sticks. I wish I had a yard to work in. And a garden. I can't wait to move to a place with some land."

"You have to be kidding. I know you said you're tired of apartment living, but I thought it meant you wanted more space. Like a villa, where they have a lawn service. Living in a house is constant work."

I took a minute to picture my life in Tampa. "I miss the condo. Someone else took care of the grounds. Maintenance men at my beck and call."

Clair raised her hands in the air. "Give me upkeep. I want to get my hands dirty. Plant flowers and vegetables. Rake leaves. Even wash windows." She skipped ahead and then twirled around to walk backwards. "I'd love to live in the country on four or five acres." Without missing a step she pivoted to face forward again. "Let's take the path down by the ravine. We haven't been that way for months."

"No way. That's where we found the dead body. I can't believe you'd want to walk past that scene."

Clair dismissed the thought with a flap of her hand. "Over and done with. We're not likely to find another body. How many murders do you think could take place in this little burg?"

"It's not that I expect another murder victim. It's the memory of the last one. Doesn't it give you the creeps?"

"I don't think about it. Don't like to keep negative things in my mind. But if it bothers you we'll take the trail past the pond instead."

Clair veered to the right and powered on, waving her hands as she spoke. "Hey guess what. I'm cooking. I bought a spaghetti squash yesterday. Going to roast it tonight."

"With your work schedule, when do you have time to cook? I didn't think you ever used your stove."

She giggled. "I had to read the instruction manual. And dust the burners. But girlfriend, my priorities are changing. I can work less, enjoy life and still earn a decent living. I'm getting out of the old race."

I wondered if her exercise priorities would change any time soon. Maybe she'd let me out of the race—this race. The longer she talked about her evolving lifestyle the faster her feet went. I changed the subject. "Have you asked Anita to join us for our power walks?"

Why was I the only friend subjected to this? Maybe the only one gullible enough?

Clair strode on. "Three's too many. It works better with two on the trail." She paused for a moment. "By the way, there's a class on gardening at the library next month. Why don't we go?"

No.

"Um, I'll think about it. You must be serious about moving. Have you looked at houses?"

"I'm keeping my eyes open. Looking at country homes that are still close to town. I don't want to be far from the office. And I need to be close to Ava's Java. We can still have our coffee meetings, although I'll probably invite you and Anita over to my house, too. Maybe I'll have a big farm kitchen."

I was happy she didn't want to change everything. Clair and I and the third member of our team, Anita, met at Ava's Java, several times a week. The coffee house was the place to discuss world affairs, local news, and what we thought of Ava's new hair-cut.

Musical notes began to drift from Clair's pocket. She pulled out her cell phone and slowed her stride while she answered.

I took the interruption in our conversation as an invitation to catch my breath and tighten my pony-tail.

Clair clicked off and stuck the cell back into her pocket. "Sorry, I wasn't going to answer it, but saw it was my boss, so I had to."

"Not a problem."

A welcome relief.

"Was it anything important? Do you need to get back to work early? I'd understand." *I really wouldn't mind.*

Clair stopped and pivoted toward me. "Something interesting. We were called by a mortgage company. It seems they have a place here in Evelynton that has gone through foreclosure. They were never able to contact the owner, so they considered it an abandoned house. Anyway, Howard said they want us to list it as soon as possible. He asked me to go over today and check it out. We have to make sure they didn't trash it. I get to decide what it will take to make it market ready. And the listing is mine. If it's in good shape it'll be an easy sale. The mortgage company only needs to recoup what's left of their investment. Howard says the price will be right."

Clair linked arms with me and slowed to a stroll. "Go with me to see it. I hope it isn't too much of a mess. This will be fun. And if it's a bore, we won't stay long. Then we'll go to Ava's for a cup."

I thought of my computer at home waiting for me to finish my latest Hoosier Lakes Living article. Hmm. What would be more enticing? I could go with my friend, or I could sit alone in my house and talk to the cat for the rest of the day. "Sure. When do you want to go?"

The good thing about being a writer—the flexible schedule. The bad thing—I take advantage of the flexible schedule. That left me rushing to meet deadlines or failing to be productive. Hence my part-time receptionist job at The Rare Curl. Twelve hours a week got me out of the house, helped to pay bills, and forced me to wear make-up. As an introvert writer, it's a challenge to wear anything but sweats, and to remember to comb my hair."

"Sometime this afternoon. I'll call you when I'm done with my appointment this morning. Howard arranged for a locksmith to open the door and change the locks. As soon as I find out it's open, I'll be over to get you."

We turned the corner and headed toward home. The sight of the little bungalow, inherited from my Aunt Ruth, drew me forward and provided renewed energy. I focused on the front porch and could taste the coffee.

I trudged up the steps and leaned into the door until it swung open.

Clair jogged in place on the sidewalk. "I'm heading home to get ready for work. I'll call you this afternoon. This should be fun unless the dead-beat owner tore out all the lighting fixtures. I'm afraid that often happens in a foreclosure. But we'll see." She jogged to her car, climbed in and squealed the tires as she sped away.

I wanted to fall onto the sofa, but forced myself to the kitchen to reheat the coffee.

Mason circled my feet until I picked him up. His purring body vibrated against my chest while I carried him to the back porch. He leapt to the floor and dashed through his cat door to the backyard.

Cradling my micro-waved coffee, I went to the shower and stripped off sweaty clothes. The bed called to me. But no, I'd find something nice to wear and even put on mascara and lipstick. Clair would be in full make-up, a painfully-tailored short-skirted business suit, and spike heels.

This was my life. Impersonating a homeless person while I wrote fluffy articles of interest only to senior citizens. The highpoint of my week would be visiting a foreclosed house.
I needed a life.

Chapter Two

Clair sat forward and tapped the steering wheel as she drove. "Every home I list is an adventure. Wondering what's it going to look like? How can I help the homeowner prepare it? What kind of person is the perfect buyer?"

I put out my hand to brace myself on the dash. She slammed on the brakes at the stop sign, looked both ways and sped on. "In the years I've been in the business I've developed a sixth sense about houses. At my first visit I get an impression of how easily it will sell and what type of person should live in it."

I lifted my chin to smile, hoping to appear as excited as my friend but only managed to sneeze. "Sorry. Being out in the park must have aggravated my sinus problem." I searched my bag for a tissue to blow my nose.

Clair turned off the car radio. "This house is special, I can tell. And I haven't even seen it yet."

I tucked the tissue back into my handbag and leaned my head back. "Just hope it isn't too dusty."

Larry's Lock and Key - 24/7 Lock-picking Service was printed on the side of the white panel truck parked in the driveway. Clair hopped out of the car and waved to the man in the driver's seat. "Hi, I'm Clair Lane from HH Realty."

The lock smith slid out of the van and ambled over to meet her as she approached. "Good afternoon, ma'am. You must be the woman I hand the keys to. Both front and back doors are re-keyed."

Clair grinned as she stuck out her hand. She'd been in this business for twenty years. Yet she behaved as if she'd won a ticket to an amusement park.

The man returned to the van and backed it out of the drive, leaving us a full view of the property.

We stood side by side, gazing at the abandoned house, me thinking it was nothing special and wishing I'd stayed home, Clair smiling while she studied the siding or the windows or the atmosphere. Or something. I didn't know what.

Without tearing her eyes from the house, she nodded. "Awesome. This is perfect."

"Really? It looks sort of ordinary to me." Newer than my Cape Cod, but a simple ranch style home.

"The siding is in great condition. The roof looks good, at least from here. Nice curb appeal. I'd add a few bushes at the end of the walk. This will be great."

I squinted, trying to see the property through Clair's eyes. "Uh-huh." Maybe I'd catch the feeling of the house once inside.

Clair scanned the yard. "I'll have to find someone to trim the shrubbery and get the leaves out of the mulch. Those beautiful leaves are falling. Too bad it's autumn, it would be easier to sell in Spring or Summer. Let's go in."

She hustled to the front door and inserted the key. Before turning the knob she twisted toward me. "I love this part. The first view of the inside is always exhilarating. I still get butterflies. You never know what to expect. I can almost hear trumpets and a drum roll."

I tried to smile. "Me too."

She turned back to the door but stopped and tipped her head toward me. "Wait. Just to clarify, this house was abandoned so we don't know what to expect. Any furniture in good condition will be gone. Sometimes the owners trash a place before leaving, even as far as pulling out light-fixtures. I hope that didn't happen but prepare yourself."

I imagined the drum roll and prepared for the cymbal clanging at the let-down when we walked into a disaster scene. The door swung open and Clair stood rooted in the entryway. I scooted in beside her hoping to catch the excitement of the first glimpse.

Her head turned as she scanned the room side to side. "No way."

We stood in the entry of a typical middle-class living room. The carpet was clean. Curtains hung in the windows. Blue and yellow pillows sat propped in the corners of a light-brown sofa. There were end tables with lamps at each side of the couch as well as beside the two upholstered chairs. A remote control sat on the coffee table. A television was nestled in an entertainment center. Nicely framed prints hung on the walls. The thought struck me that at any moment the woman of the house would appear with a plate of cookies to welcome her guests. Or maybe to ask us what the heck we were doing standing in her living-room.

I leaned toward Clair. "Are you surprised?"

Clair shrugged. "I've never seen this in a foreclosure. Sometimes, when someone is selling, they stage the house, but even if that were the case this is over-the-top. It looks as if the owner just stepped out and will be back any minute."

"We are in the correct house, right? It doesn't seem abandoned to me."

"Of course it...." Clair stopped and cut her eyes to me. "What if we have the wrong address? What if the owner returns home to find we've changed their locks? I'm calling the office."

A car engine sounded outside. Clair grabbed my arm and we both pivoted to peek out through the window. "The automobile drove past the house."

"Phew."

We stood side by side like ten-year-olds in a haunted house while Clair phoned her boss and explained the situation.

"Okay Howard. If you're sure. Yes, it will be easier to sell with furniture in it. Barely needs any staging."

She stashed her phone in her handbag. "Howard is positive this is the correct house. He double checked the address. Let's look around."

I hovered close behind Clair as she walked to the kitchen. A tea pot sat on the counter. Clair lifted the lid and pulled out a strainer. "Look at this. I thought everyone used tea bags. They could have at least cleaned it out." She moved to the sink and opened the doors underneath. "For goodness sakes, Lauren. You don't have to cling to me. I told you we're in the right place."

"Sorry. Still feel like I'm trespassing." I struck out on my own and opened cupboards. There were dishes and glassware, all clean and neatly in place. When I reached the refrigerator and pulled it open I found a different story. "Uh oh."

Clair peaked around my shoulder and pushed the door shut. "Yuk. I'll get someone to clean that out. You would think they'd have emptied the fridge before leaving."

Clair opened the dishwasher. "A few dirty dishes. At least it looks like they were rinsed first. I don't see any mold. If I run detergent through a couple of times, this will probably be fine."

She straightened and planted her hands on her hips. "It looks like they just packed up their clothes and left. Must not have been able to take the household goods."

"If I couldn't pay the mortgage I would have sold the furniture and had a garage sale. I wonder what their story was." Ideas began to flow for the plot of a short story. Were the owners spies? Drug-lords?

Clair shrugged. "People are strange. I'm going to take a look at the rest of the house."

"I'll go with you." I fell into stride behind her. In my imagination the owner stormed in and demanded to know what we were doing there. He carried an AK-47.

We crossed the living room and entered a hallway where I had to force myself to stay off Clair's heels. The first room we passed was a small bathroom. "There's a hair brush beside the sink."

Clair shook her head and muttered. "Told you every house is a new adventure. Sure haven't seen anything like this. I can't wait to tell Howard."

I followed Clair into a bedroom on the left. She glanced over her shoulder at me. I stepped back to allow space between us. "Sorry."

"This must be the master. Isn't that a pretty comforter? It even has pillows to match. Whoever defaulted on this mortgage was very accommodating in leaving all their nice things."

I patted the comforter. "Soft. It must be down."

The sound of a closet door opening and a gasp caused me to spin around. Clair, eyes round and mouth open, pointed at the open closet. Hangers filled with blouses and dresses, lined the pole. A shelf held a stack of slacks. On the floor, an array of shoes ranging from flats to dressy high-heels sat lined up against the wall.

"This is too weird." Clair rushed to the dresser and pulled open a drawer. Under garments. Another drawer. Socks and assorted hosiery.

"I'm astounded. This is the strangest listing I've ever been offered. Sure I've seen homes stuffed with belongings. But that's when the owners still lived there. I had to tell them how much to take out of the house so it would sell."

I clutched my handbag to my chest. "What happened to whoever owned this house?"

"It must be a sad story. The owner went somewhere and wasn't able to return. Still, if they were in the hospital or something Howard would have had that information."

"Why wouldn't family have come and packed it up?"

"This is beyond me. All I know is it was repossessed and my job is to sell it, so that's what I'll do."

She plopped down on the edge of the bed, took out a notebook and started scribbling notes. "I'll hire someone to clean out the personal stuff from the drawers and closets. Probably can sell a lot of it. Have to contact the mortgage company to see if they claim anything.

I started to sit beside Clair but thought better of it, not wanting to appear so comfortable in a stranger's bedroom. I couldn't shake the feeling we would soon be discovered. Instead, I crossed the hallway. There was a typical guest room with a double bed neatly made up. The closets were bare except for a few folded blankets.

When I returned to the master, Clair looked up with a smile. "I was thinking. This place is in great condition and in a prime location. I wonder if I could buy it."

My legs were tired so I leaned against the wall. "Are you kidding? It's spooky."

Clair patted the bed beside her. "For goodness sakes sit down. Nobody's coming in to chase us away. Whatever the situation with the previous owner, the house belongs to the mortgage company and they want to sell it."

I blew out a breath and sat down next to Clair. "You're right it's a nice place but I thought you wanted something in the country."

"I did. Still do but this would be a great stepping stone. I have a feeling the price will be right. I could live here until I find the right country home. Then I'll sell at a nice profit. It's an investment."

Clair stood up. "I need to take a second look around."

We walked back into the living room and Clair bounced down on the sofa slinging her arm over the side. "I like it. Can't you see me living here? Maybe have the walls painted and new carpet. It's a nice neighborhood."

I sat in a matching chair and sneezed, grabbing a tissue from my bag. "Kind of dusty. Nobody's cleaned for a while."

Clair reached out with her finger and made a swirl on the coffee table. "I'll hire a professional house cleaner as soon as we get rid of the unnecessary items."

"Hate to keep repeating myself, but I can't imagine someone walking out and leaving everything. What're they doing for a hairbrush or toothbrush for goodness sake? I didn't see any personal photos, so maybe they took those. But I'd think they would take clothes and," I picked up a bird figurine, "some of the knick-knacks. Don't you have a strange feeling about this? The owner must have had some kind of family emergency, dropped everything and left."

Clair sighed. "Former owner. It's no use wondering what happened. The mortgage company took a loss. They have an investment in the property and need to recoup it. Just remember that. Don't make up stories you don't know are true."

She kicked off her shoes and put her feet on the coffee table. "I can see my sectional in this room. It would fit perfectly. I like the coffee table. The entertainment center is dated and has to go. Most of my furniture will work fine."

I scanned the room, picturing Clair's stuff in it. "You're right. I think it would look great."

Clair put her feet down and slipped on her heels. "Haven't seen the garage yet. What kind of surprises do you suppose are stored in there?"

Chapter Three

Clair jumped to her feet and skipped through the kitchen. "I'm going to love this house."

I sneezed and followed, searching my bag for another tissue. "You're right. If you get it at a good price, this will be perfect for you. Aren't you the lucky one?"

I caught up with my friend at the doorway leading into the garage. "To me, this would be worth half the cost of the house. No more scraping ice off car windows." Clair stretched her arm into the dark room. She slapped the wall a few times in search of the light switch before she chirped, "Found it." Nothing happened.

"Clair. Isn't the electricity turned off? There's no power."

"Shoot. I knew that. It's just a habit. So, no electric light. And there aren't any windows in the garage."

"Hold on. I saw a flashlight in one of the cupboards." I retreated to the kitchen and pulled open doors. "Got it. And it works."

Clair reached out from the dark room and grabbed the flashlight. "Can't wait to get the electric garage door working. It's stuffy in here."

I watched the circle of light travel across the concrete floor.

Clair's voice now echoed from the depths of the garage. "Oh my, look at this. There's a car in here."

The light moved over a large shape that was definitely an automobile, parked in the center of the room. "What do you think it is? Looks like some sort of SUV doesn't it?"

The sphere of light dropped to the floor and I heard Clair's giggle. "Wait until I tell Howard about this listing. He's never going to believe it."

The beam of light lifted to my face. "Hey. You need to replace that old Chrysler. This looks like a late model. Maybe you could buy it cheap. What do you think?"

"It has to be better than my thirty-six-year-old station wagon. But it's sort of hard to tell with that flashlight shining in my eyes."

"Oops." The light swung away. More of the automobile came into view as Clair approached it. "Come on. Let's take a look." The interior light popped on when she pulled open the driver side door. "The battery's still good. It's sort of smelly, but looks nice. Go ahead and sit in it."

The illuminated car interior gave me the courage to venture into unknown territory, and I shuffled closer to the vehicle.

"Try it out. It's not bad." With a firm grip on my arm Clair pulled me to the open car-door.

I peeked inside. "It is a nice car. Are you sure the

mortgage company will sell it?"

"I promise you they aren't interested in used cars. Go ahead. Climb in."

"Okay. There's no denying I need better transportation. "I climbed in and tried it on for size. "Yuk, it really smells. It's going to need a good cleaning."

Clair had continued her inspection of the outside of the car. "I don't see any dings. Don't worry about the smell. It's been closed up and just needs airing out. You'll probably find a sack of old hamburgers in there."

"Umm, I think it's worse than that. You should be where I am. You aren't getting the full effect."

Clair sidestepped from window to window while I checked out the buttons on the radio. "I wonder where the owner left the keys. We could start it and see how it runs."

"I would love to have a radio without static."

Clair had reached the back of the automobile when her scream bounced off the garage walls. "What is that? Oh gosh. Lauren, get out of the car." Her high-heels scraped the concrete floor. "Get out right now!"

"No problem. I'm getting out. The smell's getting bad anyway. Even through my stuffy nose. What's the matter?" I slid out and pushed the car door shut.

Clair's voice, elevated to a higher pitch, echoed in the room. "Oh crap. Where's my phone? Lauren, do you have my phone?"

"No. What's wrong with you?" With the car interior light off, I was again watching the beam from the flashlight. It swung wildly around the room.

"My phone. Where's my phone?"

"Your cell is in your handbag isn't it? That's where you put it after you talked to Howard."

"Left it on the counter." Clair snagged my arm as she ran past, and pulled me into the house. Her grip didn't loosen until I'd been propelled to the far side of the sunny kitchen."

I rubbed red hand-prints from my arm. "What on earth? Did you see a rat or something in there? I've never seen you so white. Not since that incident in the ravine."

She twisted toward me. "Dead body. In the car."

"No way. You're playing a joke on me."

She grabbed my shoulders and pulled me to within a few inches of her face. There was no hint of a smile. "It's not a joke. There's a body in there."

"I knew it. That's what I smelled. What was it? Raccoon? Not a dog, I hope."

She released my shoulders and stalked to the living room. "No Lauren. Not an animal—a person. I'm pretty sure there was a dead woman in the cargo area. All shriveled up with its mouth wide open." Clair demonstrated with her own mouth.

"Listen, I know as soon as I believe you, you'll have a good laugh and call Anita to tell her all about how you scared me."

Clair spun to face me. "I'm not joking. Rotting corpse." She put her fingers to her eyes. "Sunken eye-sockets. Stringy hair. Dried up face."

She stopped and examined me from head to toe. "What's that smell?" She took two steps back. "Oh, man. It's you."

"You're serious? A body in the car?" I took a deep breath. "I think I smell it too."

Crap.

"It's clinging to my clothes isn't it? Crap!" I bolted for the sliding glass door and fumbled with the lock until it released. Stumbling into the yard, I stripped off my sweater. "If I fluff my shirt, maybe it'll air out."

Clair followed me outside with the cell phone clasped to her ear. "Hello 911? Hi. We have a problem."

Once she'd finished summoning the authorities, Clair turned her attention to me and wrinkled her nose. "Ugh."

I shuddered. "What am I going to do?"

Her long manicured index-finger pointed at the house. "There's a closet-full of clothes in there. Go shed yours and find something else to wear."

I gazed at the house, considering Clair's logic. It almost seemed like a good idea. "No! Those clothes belong to someone else. Probably to that dead person. Not a chance." I sniffed the sleeve of my shirt. Even my swollen sinuses couldn't block the sickening odor. "I'll move around a bit. Give the smell a chance to dissipate." I trotted to the side of the yard and back.

On my return, Clair put up a hand like a crossing guard. "Keep going."

While we waited for the whine of the sirens I entertained any neighbors, who may have been standing at their windows, by flapping my arms and running in circles.

Chapter Four

Clair returned from her third trip to scan the street. "Where are the police? They're taking forever."

"And I'm getting tired of circling the lawn. Let's go in and sit down. My clothes must be aired out by now." I left my sweater in the middle of the yard and led the way inside. Clair walked straight to the kitchen to open windows. I took the hint, and opened all the living room windows. Once a breeze was flowing, we sat on the sofa.

Clair didn't last long before she got up and moved to a side-chair. She leaned an elbow on the arm-rest with her hand covering her nose. "Gosh. Do you suppose that thing in the garage is the owner of this house?"

I shrugged, not thinking of much more than how good a shower would feel.

We stared silently into space for a few more minutes before Clair twisted to face me. "You'd think we'd be better at this since it's the second body this year."

"I thought we were going to forget about the other one. Besides, this is worse, at least for me. I want to get home and scrub myself with sanitizer. And deodorizer. Maybe I'll run through the carwash—without the car."

Sirens sounded in the distance and grew steadily louder. "Finally." Clair got up and went to the door at the sound of screeching tires from the drive-way.

She returned followed by two policemen, one of whom I was much too familiar with. I'd run into Officer Jimmy Farlow many times in the eighteen months since my return home. The encounters were never pleasant. Each time I'd ventured into the wrong place and had had terrible timing. In my opinion, the officer was overly suspicious, and always too eager to pin the blame on me. More than once he'd threatened to put me in jail.

"You know Officer Farlow, Lauren. And this is Officer Amos Smith."

Farlow stopped short at the sight of me. He closed his eyes for a moment and then focused on Clair.

I guess I wasn't high on his list of favorite people either. If ignoring me was his way of dealing, that was good enough for me. I turned my back and wandered to the sliding glass door, thankful that Clair would handle him.

"Show me this alleged body, Ms. Lane."

I glanced at them as Clair led the way into the kitchen.

Officer Smith acknowledged me with a nod and followed Farlow.

Clair showed the men to the door of the garage and stepped out of the way. "I'm staying here. You go on, but brace yourself officers. It's gruesome. And I'd advise that you don't open the car doors. You should probably just look through the windows. At least until you can get the automatic garage door open. You'll need the ventilation."

The men grinned and exchanged a look.

Farlow smirked. "Don't worry about us, ma'am. We're seasoned law enforcement and have seen our share of crime scenes. Haven't we Amos?"

I went as far as the doorway between living room and kitchen, to watch. When the men marched bravely into the garage, Clair joined me. We listened to the sound of a car door opening.

It only took about three minutes for Officer Smith's voice to be heard from the depths of the garage. "What on earth?" Clair turned eyes to me. "I warned them."

A minute later Farlow stumbled into the kitchen holding a handkerchief over his nose. "Oh mother of pearl, that's awful." We watched as his eyes lost focus.

I whispered. "Is he turning green?"

My friend and I parted to make room as he rushed between us and burst through the open door to the back yard. Officer Smith trotted along after him. Clair and I turned to see Farlow standing in the shrubbery, bent over at the waist. We averted our eyes as he made retching noises. When finished, he came up gasping for air. I couldn't blame him. No matter how many years he'd been on the job he'd only worked in Evelynton. I had a suspicion he'd never run into a case like this.

Officer Smith fared better. He circled the backyard taking deep cleansing breaths.

The two gained strength and returned to the house. "Amos, we'll have to call the chief and the cor...."

Ugh." Farlow pivoted and stumbled through the sliding door once again.

A few minutes later he returned with his phone to his ear. Clicking it off, he maintained his composure. "The chief says he'll take care of notifying all the proper departments."

Farlow put his hand on the notebook always stowed in his pocket. Before he could pull it out his skin-color paled and he trudged toward the backyard. "Let's go out here while I take your statements." The officer took deep breaths, looking as if he was preparing for natural childbirth. He breathed in and blew out, while Clair filled him in on all the particulars. My friend was good at sticking to the facts and seldom got herself into trouble. Unfortunately one of the facts was that I'd been inside the car.

"Ms. Halloren, why did you enter the automobile with the body?"

Crap.

"Obviously I didn't know there was a body. If I'd known I wouldn't have gotten near it." I paused to calm myself and adjust my attitude. "Clair mentioned the car might be for sale and I need one. I only sat in the front seat and didn't notice the odor at first."

I tapped my nose. "Allergies or a cold has had me stuffed up. It took a couple of minutes before the smell penetrated." I glanced toward the house. "I never want to see a used car again. My Chrysler may be old, but at least I know there isn't corpse in it."

Farlow began to sway and turned his attention to the shrubbery. With a wave of his hand he said, "You two can go. Show up at the station later this afternoon to finish your statements." He edged toward the bushes and we dashed for the door.

We power-walked through the living room to the front door and ran for the car. Clair pushed buttons that lowered all the windows.

On the way home I couldn't help but giggle. "Poor Jimmy Farlow. He was absolutely green. Bet he was mortified when he got sick. I hope he didn't get anything on his perfect uniform. He'll have to take it to the drycleaner."

"He's always been so professional. Do you suppose he's ever vomited at a crime scene before? I bet he's swearing Amos to secrecy right now."

"He couldn't even keep it together long enough to write in his trusty notebook." A wave of remorse hit me. "Let's quit making fun of him. He tries so hard."

"You're right. I'll change the subject." Clair grinned and tipped her head toward me. "Do you still want me to inquire about buying the car? I bet you'll get it really cheap, now. Maybe free."

I cut my eyes to Clair. "Very funny. I'd rather ride a bike."

~~

Clair pulled to the curb in front of my house on Stoneybridge, to let me out.

My trusty feline friend, Mason, sat inside the front door, waiting to greet me. I reached down to take him into my arms but he crouched out of my reach. Hair stood up on his back and his nose twitched as he crept toward me. Then my loyal companion, who needed reminding that I'd rescued him from life on the street, spun around and fled the room. Claws scraped the hardwood floor as he steaked into the dining room.

"Oh come on. A little support here. It can't be that

bad." The cat flattened himself to the floor and peeked out from under the dining room table. "Well, it's sort of bad." I stripped off my clothes in the kitchen and stuffed them into a garbage bag destined for the trash, before running for the shower. It took two shampoos, and scrubbing every inch of skin with a loofah, before I felt presentable to the cat, let alone the rest of the world.

When I returned to the living room Mason cautiously inspected me before he welcomed me home. There was no telling how the rest of Evelynton would receive me, after word got out.

Chapter Five

A full night in bed and I was still exhausted. Had I even slept? Oh, yes. It was all too clear. I'd slept enough to experience several frantic dreams. Each vision featured a new dead body. The last turned out to be a nightmarish adventure and I recalled every minute of it.

I sang to the radio as I drove my vintage station wagon along a murky country road. That I sang The Monster Mash should have alerted that it something was up. But I happily warbled until I glanced to my right. I wasn't alone in the Chrysler. A shriveled and blackened corpse occupied the passenger seat. When I noticed the uninvited guest seemed to be wearing my sweater, I screamed and the steering wheel spun. We—that's me and the ghoulish figure beside me—careened off the road, bounced down an embankment, and landed in a thorn bush. If I thought the dead passenger was scary, there was worse to come. Illuminated by the headlights, Officer Farlow stood front and center, glaring at me. It was that sight that woke me. My heart thumped and the stench of decay filled my nostrils.

As I laid in bed, calming myself, my brain told me the smell was only in the dream. But my nose wasn't convinced. Back in the shower, I successfully removed another layer of skin, finished with an application of lavender scented lotion and a healthy coating of hair-spray. I don't often use hair-spray. My hair usually does what it wants, but the added flowery scent couldn't hurt. I thought I might make standing three feet away from people a rule for the day.

When I made it to the kitchen, perfumed and dressed, Mason glanced at me from beside his food dish. "Good morning. Where were you last night? I was expecting you to keep my feet warm."

The cat stared at his empty food dish.

Taking the hint, I rummaged in the closet for the cat food. "Where did you sleep?"

Mason lifted his chin to gaze into space, ignoring me as only a feline could. "Oh come on, the odor is gone. Everything back to normal."

I filled his dish with kibble and carried my coffee to the dining table. When my judgmental pet finished eating, he silently padded into the room and circled me. "I know cats have a keen sense of smell, but…" He relaxed and sat on my foot. A quiet gesture of acceptance.

~~

I stood outside The Rare Curl while I counted to ten, not sure what reaction might await me inside. After spending the entire night reliving the previous day, recounting it to anyone seemed like agony. But pretending the events didn't happen wouldn't fly either. Word would have seeped between the cracks of the police department walls and circulated through town before lights-out last night. It would have been the prime topic of conversation over every plate of bacon and eggs that morning.

I grabbed the door and charged in. Rarity stood beside her styling station and flashed a cheerful welcoming smile. "Good morning, Lauren. How are you this lovely morning? Did you have a nice day off?"

No urgent requests as to the state of my well-being? No "Tell me all about it."

Could it be that my boss was unaware of the gruesome find? Was I wrong about Evelynton's wagging tongues? No, the more accurate answer would be Rarity was the one person in town who actively avoided gossip. One of her favorite sayings was something about, without wood a fire goes out.

She plopped down in a waiting room chair and pushed her hair from her face. "The phone's been ringing all morning, but I was knee-deep in floor cleaner in the supply room, so I let it go to voice-mail. Thank goodness it's your day to work. I knew you'd take care of the messages. Sorry, there are probably a lot of them."

She flashed a grin. "Good news, though. I've hired a new hairdresser and she will be able to help you with the desk until she builds her client list. You'll get to know her later this week."

"That's exciting. I look forward to meeting her. But there's something you should know before anyone else comes in."

I sank into the chair next to Rarity. "Yesterday was a strange day. You'll hear the story soon enough." Rarity gave me her full attention as I related the string of events leading to the horrific discovery.

Sometime during the conversation, Stacy slipped in and stood near us. When she'd heard enough, she hissed, "It was you! You found the mummified woman? My friend Irma—she works at the police station—called me this morning. It's so exciting." Stacy leaned toward me—close enough I could feel her breath. "What'd it look like? Was it scary? How gross was it?" Evelynton's gossip mill had lived up to my expectations.

Rarity glanced at Stacy. "I'm sure the experience must have been troubling for Lauren. Let's not hash over the gory particulars."

"Okay. Sorry." Stacy nodded and stood up straight. A few seconds later, she'd returned her attention to me. "Do you know who it was? They said it was a female, but Irma didn't hear a name. She couldn't hear much through the closed office door. Only caught bits of information." Stacy lowered her voice. "What can you tell me?"

I shook my head. "I don't have any idea of the woman's identity. The house was supposed to be vacant. That's all I know."

Stacy planted her hands on her hips. "Okay. They said they think it was the owner of the house. The body was almost mummified. It must have been there at least six months, maybe longer. Just think, in the back of the car all that time."

Rarity shook her head. "The poor woman. Maybe she was cleaning the car and had a heart attack or an episode of some kind."

Stacy sucked in a deep breath. "I bet she committed suicide. Let the motor run. Then went to the back to lie down and wait for the carbon monoxide to get her. She was probably alone and depressed. Happens all the time."

Stacy took a minute to stare into space. "Can you imagine? Then the body just laid there."

That troubled me. "They said she'd been there six months? Why didn't anyone report her missing? No one checked on her? Where was her family? Where were her friends?"

I thought back to when my husband had been killed by a stray bullet in Tampa. I'd shut everyone out. If I'd died, how long would my body have lain unattended in the condo? I wouldn't have been found until the rent was overdue, or the smell seeped through the walls.

Ick.

Rarity clenched the cross pendant she always wore. "It's such a sad story. The Bible says 'Two are better than one.' And even has the warning. 'Woe to him who falls when he is alone. He has no one to lift him up.' That's in Ecclesiastes."

Stacy and I observed a moment of silence.

I twisted toward Stacy. "Wait. If she committed suicide, it couldn't have been with car exhaust. The keys weren't in the ignition. I didn't see them anywhere."

"Huh." She walked to her styling station and pulled out her supplies for the day. "Must have done it some other way. Shot herself? Took pills?"

"Did Irma say whether or not they found a gun?"

"Oh. No."

Stacy waved her hands and rushed back. "I forgot to tell you. The mummy was holding a flower—all dried up—in her hand. Weird isn't it? That's sort of why I thought it was suicide."

My boss and I asked simultaneously, "What kind of flower?" I don't know why that seemed to matter.

"I don't know. Like I said, it was dried up. Same condition as the body."

Stacy stared into my eyes. "I know. The mummy lady took poison and laid herself out in the back seat with a flower in her hand. Then she waited to die."

Rarity stood and planted her hands on her hips. "Let's offer respect to the deceased and not refer to her as the mummy lady. And please refrain from speculation today. There will be enough of that from our customers. Be assertive and steer the conversations to more pleasant subjects."

"You're right. We don't need to add to the gossip." I moved to my desk.

"Alright." Stacy shuffled to the coffee pot.

I studied the appointment book but couldn't get the mummy, umm, deceased out of my mind. The woman who'd died with no one to care. She'd dropped out of sight and no one missed her. Sad thoughts swirled through my head for the remainder of my shift. By the time I left the salon, I could barely walk under the weight of it. I turned to my one refuge, Ava's Java. The jovial proprietor's friendly smile was always a welcome sight.

I visited the coffee shop several times a week. Would Ava notice if I disappeared? If no one saw me for a week, for two or three weeks, would anyone miss me?

"Rarity would miss me." I said to no one. But what if I didn't have the part-time job? Who then? An old loneliness began to surface.

"Lauren!" A voice bubbled from my favorite table

near the window.

What was I thinking? Anita brought me back to reality. I couldn't ask for a more reliable friend. The woman was on the phone if I was fifteen minutes late for a coffee date. If she didn't get an answer she'd be pounding on my door. Clair might take longer to notice my absence, but sooner or later she'd look for me, too. I settled my mug on the table, pulled up a chair, and eased into it to bask in the glow of friendship. I whispered, "Thank you God." There were at least three people in the world who would notice if I dropped out of sight.

Friends. There was a time when I didn't have any. An introvert by temperament, depression had forced me further into seclusion. It was only my necessary move back to Evelynton that brought me out of the imagined safety of solitude. And then only after Anita and Clair aggressively inserted themselves into my daily schedule.

Anita gazed into my eyes and shook her head. "Clair called this morning and filled me in on the events. What an ugly experience. I couldn't believe she made you get into the car. Of course I'm sure that was before she realized there was a corpse was in the backseat."

I pulled at my collar. "I keep imagining I can smell it. Even had nightmares last night."

Anita stretched over table and sniffed. "I don't smell anything. Except your perfume. It smells nice. Is it new?"

She clasped her coffee cup with both hands. "How do you suppose the poor woman was in there, dead, for so long without anyone realizing? What about her family? Her friends?"

"That's what I've been wondering all morning. I guess there was no one who cared enough to look for her."

"Hard to believe it happened here. This is Evelynton, for goodness sake. I thought everybody knew everyone's business."

Anita sipped her coffee before beginning again. "What about her bills?" She ticked off her fingers. "Lights? Gas? House payment? Car payment? Shouldn't someone have noticed her mail piling up?"

"The electricity was off when we got there. It had been out long enough for the food in the refrigerator to rot. I didn't see any mail."

My friend leaned back in her chair and eyed me. "This is quite a mystery. And what's the story going around? She held a flower in her hand? I think it's a job for the Danger Girls Detective Agency. Let's go over and question the neighbors. I bet they know something. We could break the case wide open."

I leveled my gaze at Anita. "There is no Danger Girls Detective Agency. I'm a writer not a detective. And you are a contented housewife. At least you were before you got involved with me."

"You're only hesitant because you almost got shot those other times. There's no danger of that here. The woman's been dead for—what did they estimate—six months to a year, at least?"

Anita threw her hands in the air. "Let's do it. This will be an adventure, and it will be safe."

My resolve wavered. "It's true the risk, if there ever was one, is in the past. I admit it's intriguing."

I began to mentally list questions I'd ask the

neighbors. "Hold on. There's another problem. I've been warned repeatedly to stay out of police business. There might not be a risk of being shot, but there would be one of me being thrown into jail."

Anita studied me as she stirred her coffee. "Still, I know you're curious. And you can't be arrested for doing an interview." She flashed a smile. "If nothing else, this could give you the plot for your true crime novel."

"No. You know I've given that up. I have no talent for recognizing criminals. I always pick the wrong one."

I tried to ignore Anita's prodding. I wanted to be excited about going home to write travel articles, so I fixed my eyes on the traffic outside the window.

Anita was quiet.

Unable to resist, I glanced back. Blue eyes stared at me. The woman didn't blink. "Okay. I am curious about the story. I guess it wouldn't hurt to speak to a neighbor or two."

Anita slurped the last of her coffee and grinned. "You're off work for the day, right? I'm open until dinner time."

"Now? I should go home and finish—"

"Oh, come on. I want to go now. You can write later." She reminded me of a twelve year old. I didn't know any pre-teens but imagined that's how one would sound if I told them they couldn't go to a party.

"Okay. I can't be arrested for talking. We'll visit two of the neighbors. If we don't learn anything, that'll be the end of it."

Chapter Six

I shielded my eyes from the sun as I studied the victim's small white house. Anita climbed out of her mini-van and hustled around to stand beside me. "No squad cars or forensic vans. It looks as if the police have finished with it already. Want to see if we can get in?"

I whipped my gaze to Anita. "No! Are you crazy? There is still crime scene tape across the door. Besides, there's the trespassing thing."

She shrugged. "Okay. I just wanted to see it. You and Clair got to."

"It's a normal house. Nothing to see."

"Humph."

Anita pointed her chin to the house on the right, then to the house on the left. "Lauren Halloren, super crime fighter, which neighbor do we interview first?"

I scowled at Anita. "Stop that. I'm not a crime fighter."

She shrugged. "Okay. But you're the one with experience. Two cases solved in the year and a half since you've been back in Evelynton."

"Once again, I didn't solve anything. Almost got killed is what I did. If Wallace hadn't been there the first time, Patsy would have gotten away and we never would have known who killed the insurance man. And if Deloris's mobility scooter hadn't stalled, they would have found my body in the alley beside the pharmacy. If Jack hadn't intervened, I'd be in jail. My experience is filled with close-calls."

"Sure, sure. I've heard your excuses, but the whole town knows you brought down two theft rings and two murderers."

"They do not." I leveled my eyes at my friend. "A few misguided souls choose to believe I did it."

"Uh-huh." She swung to the right and then to the left. "So which house do we go to first?"

I pointed to the right. "This way." The house was almost identical to the house with the crime scene tape. I expected it to be the same layout. The garage was on the right side, with what seemed to be living room windows on the opposite end of the home. The only difference I could detect was blue siding instead of white.

Anita hurried to reach the door ahead of me, and hissed over her shoulder. "Let me do the talking this time."

"Go ahead. You're the one people love to talk to." She'd been able to discover critical information in our last escapade.

She pressed the doorbell, and within a few minutes the door opened revealing a woman of about our age. She wore loose fitting jeans and long sleeved t-shirt. "What can I do for you?" She cocked her head and looked closely at Anita. "Don't I know you? You go to the same church I do, don't you?"

"That's right, though we've not actually been introduced. This is a happy coincidence." Anita grabbed the woman's hand and introduced us.

The woman pulled her hand from my friend's grip. "Tonya Becker. Nice to meet you."

"I can't believe we haven't met before this. I try to get to know everyone at church."

Tonya flapped a hand. "Oh, my husband and I leave right after the service. Don't stay around for coffee time. We have too much to do on Sundays. You know, taking care of the yard and the house."

"I can understand that. It's never-ending."

"My husband works well over forty hours a week at Justice Insurance Company. I'm a cook at the school cafeteria. Four hours a day, but I have my housework to do."

Anita leaned on the door frame and looked genuinely interested. "You get to work with the kids. I bet that's fun. I've wondered, do you cook the meals at the school, or are they shipped in?"

"We cook 'em. One of the few cafeterias that still do."

Why had I agreed to let Anita talk? We'd be there all day. I smiled at Tonya and bumped my elbow into Anita's ribs—gently.

My talkative friend glanced at me. "Silly me, I almost forgot why we stopped by. And I don't want to take up too much of your time. Would you mind if we stepped in for a minute? We want to ask you about your neighbor." She tipped her head to the left, in the direction of the dead woman's house."

Tonya raised her eyebrows. "Oh. Of course, come

in. That was a surprise wasn't it? Never thought anything like that would happen in Evelynton, let alone in this neighborhood."

She led the way to a comfortable and well-used living room.

Anita and I took seats side by side on the brown corduroy sofa. T0nya sat in a blue plush chair across from us. I guessed it was her usual spot, since it was surrounded by fashion magazines, a paperback, an empty coffee cup, and tissues.

Tonya's eyes were bright as she leaned forward. "I have to tell you it was a shock when the police showed up over there. Can't believe that poor woman died right next door. And her body had been laying there for who knows how long."

Anita nodded. "Incredible. Did you know her well?"

"No, didn't know her at all. I'd met her of course, since she was right next door. But that's as far as it went. Can't even remember what she said her name was." Tonya scrunched her forehead. "Valerie? Victoria? Something like that. Don't remember the last name, either. It sounded foreign. Anyway, I hardly ever saw her out. My husband and I talked about that. Thought she must travel a lot. We'd see the curtains open and shut, lights on at night. You know, normal stuff for a week or so. Then no movement at the windows and no lights, so we figured she was gone on a trip. There was never much activity around the house."

"No kidding? Didn't anyone check on her house during the times she was away?"

Tonya shook her head. "Not that I saw. Well, she did have a lawn guy who showed up every week or so to mow the lawn. He took care of the leaves in the fall. He was there pretty regularly, so I we figured everything was okay. Wish we could afford a lawn guy. Yard work is about all we get done on weekends."

Anita smiled. "Oh girl, wouldn't that be heaven? I don't mind mowing in the spring but by mid-summer I've had enough."

"You and me both." The two women laughed.

Tonya glanced out the window for a moment. "Then the lawn guy must have quit about two months ago. The grass was a foot high when we realized something was up. It looked awful. My husband, Lance, started mowing it when he did ours. As if he had time."

Anita shook her head. "That's all he needed. More yard to mow."

Tonya leaned forward and nodded. "And snow to shovel this winter. It isn't good to have a house next door that appears vacant."

"I hadn't thought of that."

Tonya sighed and continued. "Well after a while Lance wised up and talked to Frank, the neighbor on the other side. He's a good guy and they started taking turns mowing. I was waiting for that woman to get back, to let her know her hired man wasn't doing his job." She gazed through the window for a moment before returning her attention to us. "I guess she won't be coming home."

I squirmed in my seat, my self-control getting away from me. So far, I'd let Anita do all the talking. Finally, I couldn't stay quiet. "Did you notice anything out of the ordinary in the last few months? I mean besides the lawn."

"No. Except her outside light burned out. It was

one of those dusk to dawn lights, but it doesn't work anymore. Lance and I've been talking about taking it on ourselves to replace the bulb. Wouldn't cost much and it would be safer in the neighborhood if all the homes had lights at night. I guess, when they sell the house, that will be fixed."

"You said there wasn't much activity at the house. Did she have visitors?"

"No, I never saw anyone. I don't think she had company the entire time she lived here. But it's not like I watched out the window all the time. I have work to do in my own home."

"Did you think it was strange she'd been gone so long this time? Did you ever report it to the police?"

Tonya shook her head. "No, Lance said we shouldn't call the police. What if she returned and found out we'd turned her in? I didn't appreciate her letting the lawn go, but Lance said it was her business what she did."

There were probably more questions I should have asked but I couldn't think of them. For a close neighbor, Tonya knew little about the dead woman. "Thank you for talking to us. We couldn't believe something like this would happen in our town, and were curious."

Anita regained control of the interview. "If you think of anything, or see anything going on over there, would you call me?" Anita pulled a business card from her purse. "Here's my number."

We stood and Anita grabbed Tonya's hand again. "I'm so glad I met you and I'll look for you at church. Maybe I can convince you and Lance to stay for coffee after the service and meet a few people."

Tonya gave a tight lipped smile and nodded.

As soon as the door closed I shot a gaze at Anita. "You have business cards? Why? I don't even have one and I'm self-employed."

"I had them printed. They say Anita Corbin, Housewife. Friend in Time of Need. Call anytime." My friend giggled. "We should have Danger Girls Detective Agency cards printed. We can get them on the Internet."

"No. Don't even think about it." I turned and led the way down the sidewalk, past the deceased woman's house.

Anita put her hand out. "Give me your notebook. We should record the information Tonya gave us."

I pulled the purse-sized notepad from my handbag and handed it to Anita. She planted her feet and scribbled notes while I studied at the foreclosed house. The house the mortgage company considered deserted, but its owner hadn't left. She'd lain entombed, waiting to be discovered.

Chapter Seven

Anita tucked my notebook into her handbag. "Isn't it odd Tonya didn't remember her neighbor's name? I'd want to know who lived next door, wouldn't you?"

"You get along with everybody. I guess it's different for someone who's lived in the same town their whole life. Until last year I never saw a need to meet the neighbors." In the city and especially in condos, it seemed prudent to avoid getting involved. Or maybe that was just me.

I'd discovered, since my return, there might have been support when my husband had been killed. Maybe if I'd known my neighbors or belonged to a church, someone would have made it a point to check on me. There were no visits. No meals delivered. My few acquaintances quit coming around when I was not communicative. One of the things that struck me about this little town was that people cared and found ways to help anyone who had trouble. At least I thought that until we found the mummy in the car.

I focused my attention on the house to the left of

the crime scene—if it was a crime scene.

Anita pushed ahead of me again and punched the doorbell. I stood close behind, on tiptoes, peering over her shoulder. The door opened and we were greeted by a tiny woman with a familiar face. Her eyes met mine.

"Hello there. Halloren, isn't it?"

I crowded around Anita and stuck out my hand. "This is a surprise. I didn't know you lived here."

Irma, the file clerk at the police station, gave my hand a vigorous shake. She flashed a vibrant smile, for a woman of her age—whatever age that was. I remembered, from our last meeting, I'd been continually adjusting my estimate of her chronological age. At different times during the conversation I'd guessed her anywhere between forty and seventy. I made a mental note to learn more about Irma.

After introducing Anita, I got cut out of the conversation. She'd nudged me out of the way and gushed over Irma like a long-lost cousin.

"Wait a minute. We met briefly at Ava's Java. Clair Lane and I were having coffee and you stopped by our table. I think you'd sprained your ankle. How are you doing with it?"

"Went to school with Clair? I remember you. My ankle is much better. Thanks for asking. Had to have it wrapped for a while."

It was going to kill me if Anita and Irma got into a long conversation. I jumped in. "Irma works at the police department. She does the filing, I think. Is that right?"

"That's correct. Been serving the station, and the citizens of Evelynton, for ten years. What brings you out on this lovely day?"

I put on my sad face. "We were talking about what happened to the poor woman next door. The discovery brought up so many questions. Anita and I wondered what her neighbors could tell us."

Irma leaned out of the doorway and scanned the street in both directions. "Come inside."

I knew the police department employee wasn't technically allowed to share information about official business. But from our previous meeting, I remembered Irma was proud of her position. Being in-the-know about crime in Evelynton, came with a certain status.

We followed Irma down a hall to her bright white kitchen. Sunshine flowed through windows bordered by yellow curtains. We sat at a table covered with a cheerful red and white checkered cloth. The diminutive file clerk pulled her chair close and leaned in. "I'm treading on dangerous territory by talking to you."

"I understand. And honestly, we had no idea you lived here. I would never want to take advantage of your friendship to gain confidential information. But since we're here...."

Irma nodded. "Good. And you should be aware I won't divulge any facts that might affect the integrity of the investigation. Make sure you don't spread any rumors that might get back to Chief Stoddard. If he thinks I spoke out of line, it could mean my job."

I made a show of shaking my head. "Never. And I can vouch for Anita. She is completely reliable to keep sensitive information to herself."

At least I hoped so.

Anita regained her position as interviewer. "Did you know the woman who lived next door?"

"Nope. Saw her outside once in a while. Oh, I

waved but never spoke to her. She didn't behave like she wanted to be neighborly, and I had things to do. Everybody around here thought she must have traveled a lot. Maybe it was part of her job. I'm sure Tonya told you that. Saw you over at her door."

"Yes she did. Wasn't anyone in the neighborhood acquainted with the deceased?"

"I doubt it. Never saw her talking to anybody around here. She was just somebody who occupied the house. Course, I know more about her now." Irma caught my eye and raised a brow.

I took the hint. "What have the police discovered?"

"Chief Stoddard wouldn't even tell me her name. Me, her neighbor. He was afraid it would get into the paper. As long as I've worked there, you'd think I'd deserve more consideration."

Anita and I nodded our agreement. "Ten years."

Irma put her arms on the table and clasped her hands. "But since you asked, I'll let you in on the little information I've gleaned from talk around the station. We're not releasing this to the public, so keep it to yourselves."

Anita made a motion as if zipping her lips.

"So what I do know is the woman lived alone. Single. Thirty-eight years old. They figure she was self-employed, or she had a lot of money. They haven't found any pay stubs or work record, but her bank statements indicate she had upwards of fifty thousand dollars in the bank at one time."

Anita blurted. "That's a lot of money. You said 'at one time' so how much is in there, now?"

"Zilch. Nada. The money ran out three months ago."

"No kidding? What happened to it?"

"I suppose living happened. She had all her bills paid electronically through the bank and eventually that used up all the money."

My attention drifted while I gazed through Irma's kitchen window. How much of her neighbor's house could she see from there?

When I returned my attention to the table, both women were staring at me. "What?"

Irma sighed and tipped her head to the side. "Weren't you listening?"

It seemed to stretch Irma's patience, but she brought me up to speed. "I said I wouldn't trust the bankers with paying my bills. I'd rather write the checks myself."

She leaned back in her chair and crossed her arms. "Then I asked Anita what she thought about it. She lets her husband take care of the bills. Now we're waiting for your opinion."

"Oh. Sorry." I shook my head to clear it. "I hadn't thought about it. There's never been a reliable balance in my bank account, so I wouldn't want to worry the bankers with it."

Irma squinted at me and returned her attention to Anita. "Anyway, the fifty-thousand kept the mortgage paid, and the lights on until the account ran dry. We, here in the neighborhood, didn't know any of this of course. Just noticed one day the lawn hadn't been mowed and pretty soon the porch light wasn't on. Course Tonya and I figured the bulb burnt out. Talked about fixing it 'cause we like lights on at night. We still thought the woman would be back to take care of it. My husband, Frank, and Tonya's Lance, took turns mowing the lawn. Believe me, they were going to pounce on the situation as soon as she got back home. Didn't take them more than an extra half hour to do her yard, but you should've heard them complain."

Anita leaned back and put her hand to her cheek. "That's amazing. All her bills were getting paid, and she could have been dead for—how long ago do the police think she died?"

"Melvin didn't say. I know the coroner made a guess at six months but wouldn't pinpoint T.O.D."

Irma glanced at Anita. "That's official talk for time of death."

"Is it?" Anita pulled out my notebook to jot that information down, then glanced up at Irma. "Do they know how she died?"

"Last I heard no one had a clue. The state guys will have to work on it and maybe figure it out in a few months. Chief Stoddard said we may never know."

Irma relaxed her arms, seemingly forgiving my lapse in attention. "He mentioned she could have killed herself. Maybe sat in the car while it was running. The garage would have filled up with carbon monoxide pretty quick."

I flashed back to the conversation with Stacy and almost corrected Irma.

She continued. "But they discovered there was still gas in the tank and the ignition wasn't on. Not even a key in the vehicle. So that theory went out the window."

Irma tapped herself on the head. "Course, I thought the flower in her hand lent itself to the suicide theory."

Anita's attention was riveted on Irma. "A flower?"

Irma nodded. "Yep. Hands clasped in front of her,

like this." She showed us with her own hands. "Holding a dried up flower. Weird isn't it?"

I almost blurted out I'd already heard that tidbit, but again thought before I spoke. If Irma knew Stacy had been talking to me, she might become wary of sharing more information.

Irma jabbed at me with her index finger. "Farlow figured she probably had a heart attack, but thought better of it. He realized she probably wouldn't have looked so peaceful. And why would she be holding the posy? Then he came up with the brilliant conclusion she shot herself. But even I could see that didn't happen. Where'd the gun go?"

Anita scribbled in my notebook again and glanced up. "Right, where did the gun go?"

Anita was taking her interviewer role seriously. "What about murder? Have they looked into that?"

Irma blinked. "Of course they looked into that. They're cops. That's what they think of first. Farlow told me there weren't any obvious injuries. Couldn't see a bullet hole, although with the corpse all dried and sort of hard, the hole would have shriveled-up." She held up her fingers forming a tiny hole. "And it didn't appear her head had been bashed in, like if she'd been hit with a blunt instrument."

Anita dropped the pen and put both hands to her face. "Head not bashed in? That's good. You said she was dried up? Shriveled?"

"Yep. Like an old mummy. Amos said she looked sort of like beef-jerky." Irma slapped the table and laughed.

"Jerky?" My friend pressed back in her seat as far as she could, then slid her chair a couple of inches away from the table. "Eew."

I could tell Anita was letting her imagination get away from her.

I touched her shoulder. "You okay?"

She whispered. "Shriveled up mummy. Beef-jerky?"

"Didn't Clair tell you about what she saw?" Anita gave a slight shake of her head and pressed her lips together.

Time to leave. Anita needed air.

"Irma, thanks for talking to us. We won't take up any more of your time."

Anita's stride wasn't perfectly steady on the way to the mini-van. She veered off course once and had to be guided back to the sidewalk. As soon as we reached the van she leaned against the door.

"Are you alright? Do you want me to drive?"

Anita straightened. "No. I just needed a minute." After some deep breaths, she managed a question. "If it was so long ago, and if the body was dri—in that condition, how will they determine what happened? You know about these things. What do you think happened to her?"

"I don't know about these things. The best I can do is guess, but I don't agree with the suicide theory. There would have been a note or some sort of clue."

I took a moment to think. "I guess she could have poisoned herself and then crawled into the car to die. And maybe she didn't leave a note because she didn't have any friends who cared."

Anita had recovered. "You're right, it could have been poison. But why would she decide to do it in the back of her SUV? If it was me, I'd want to be comfortable. Probably get into bed and pull the covers up so I'd look peaceful when they found me."

I stared at Anita for a moment. Couldn't imagine her ever entertaining a suicidal thought. "I guess it would be a way to keep from being found right away. But why worry about that if no one ever visited? Most likely she died of a natural cause and she happened to be in the back seat of the car."

Anita rolled her eyes. "And she just happened to have a flower in her hand?" She'd obviously lowered her estimate of my detective skills. "I think it was murder. Someone killed her and stuffed the body into the car to hide it."

We both stood silent for a minute.

Anita glanced at me. "That doesn't explain the flower, either."

I shook my head. "No. Had to be suicide. This is Evelynton. We don't have murders."

Anita blew out a breath and pulled the car door open. "You're right. There were those two times, but they were flukes. What are the chances we'd have a third killing in this little town?"

"Slim to none." I laughed and crawled into the passenger side. "We've been over-thinking it."

Anita turned the ignition. "You're right, we are being silly. Call Clair and see if she has time to join us for lunch."

Chapter Eight

"Great. We missed the lunch rush." Anita snagged a prime parking spot at Burgers 'n Bean Sprouts. The trendy little restaurant was carved from a 60's era filling station and gave the impression Richie Cunningham and his crew might at arrive any time.

"They make the best burgers in town, even better than Jake's." Anita's eyes got big. "Oh. Please don't tell him I said that. I let him believe his hamburgers on the grill are my favorite, and I wouldn't want to discourage his cooking."

Red vinyl seats creaked as we settled into a booth, close enough to the window to watch for Clair. We didn't have long to wait. Her black BMW kicked up dust as it flew into the lot. Two minutes later she was out of the car and striding through the door.

Anita leaned an elbow on the table. "Explain to me how she does that in high heels. I couldn't get up that much speed even in my sneakers."

Clair tossed her purse into the booth and slid in. "Glad you called, girls. I'm starved."

Our waitress, a fresh-faced, auburn-haired teen,

passed out menus. "Hey Mrs. Corbin."

"Hi Tina. Love the skirt and the headband."

"Thanks. We're supposed to dress like the 1960's. I had to google it." Tina took a breath, ready to launch into her waitress routine. She lifted a menu and pointed to the top left-hand side. "Let me draw your attention to a new menu item. We now offer veggie burgers. Totally meat-free."

Anita scrunched her forehead. "What do they taste like?"

Tina cast a quick glance toward the kitchen and whispered. "I don't know. I don't eat anything green. The manager said I have to try one so I can be knowledgeable on all our offerings, but so far I've avoided it."

A man, who might have been Tina's boss, stepped out of the kitchen to wipe the counter. Our waitress produced a big smile and raised her voice. "Everyone tells me they're quite tasty."

"My two friends and I dipped our heads to study our menus.

Anita ordered a beef burger with everything and an order of curly fries. "But no sprouts. And a cola, please."

"As tempting as a green burger is, I'll have a grilled turkey with mayonnaise and bean sprouts. And lemonade to drink."

Clair put down her menu. "Cheese burger with everything, no sprouts. Curly fries and a vanilla milkshake."

"Good choice." Tina gathered the menus and returned to the kitchen.

Anita crossed her arms over her chest and leveled

her gaze at Clair. "You never eat like that. What's going on? Are you in a stressful situation? Are you eating to satisfy emotional craving?"

Clair twisted to face Anita. "Emotional craving? What magazine have you been reading this week? I'm hungry." She shrugged. "And didn't have much breakfast."

When Anita continued to stare, Clair relented. "Maybe a little depressed, that's all. It's about the house. The transaction should've been quick and easy. I even visualized where my furniture would go. Didn't I, Lauren? Now the sale will be tied up in red-tape forever, all because we found the body. Who knows how long it will take? Why can't they just get on with it?"

I shook my head. "You still want that house? After…"

Clair shrugged. "Of course I do. The home is fine. Everything, you know the corpse and smell, was contained in the car. I'll have the garage fumigated."

"That's for bugs, like termites."

"Okay, I'll have them do whatever they do to deodorize it. With the deal I'll get on the house, I can have the interior painted and replace the carpet. It'll be great—just like new."

Anita cringed. "It sounds kind of creepy, to me."

Clair leaned back and raised her eyebrows. "Have you ever researched the history of your house? I bet we'd all be shocked to discover what's gone on in the buildings we live in. Especially the older places." Clair directed her gaze to me. "Like your little Cape Cod. How do you know someone didn't die there—or get murdered—before your aunt Ruth bought it? Maybe there are ghosts. Have you seen any mysterious lights drift past you in the night? Heard any odd thumping in the attic or footsteps on the stairs?"

"Stop it. I'm not afraid of ghosts. There's no such thing."

Crap. Now, when I woke up at three in the morning, I'd have something to stew over.

Clair's chuckle was interrupted by Tina delivering our drinks. The girl returned to the counter and almost collided with a frantic red-haired woman who had rushed in from outside. "I phoned in a to-go order. The name's Peabody."

I twisted in my seat to call to her. "Hey Rarity. This is a surprise. You must have had a large gap in your schedule in order to drive out here for lunch."

"Oh, hi girls." Rarity walked over to our booth. "I did have a cancellation but I normally wouldn't usually venture all the way out here. Wallace loves their food, so I'm picking something up for him."

Clair took a quick sip of her shake. "You're delivering his lunch? Now that is true love. The two of you have been dating for quite a while. When are you going to marry him?"

A blush crept up Rarity's neck. "He is a dear man. I don't know what I'd do without him, but we're only good friends."

My neighbor, Wallace Binion, had been reliably self-sufficient. He was always the one to offer help, not request it. I couldn't picture him asking Rarity to go out of her way. "I'm surprised he's letting you get his lunch for him. Is he sick?"

"I'm a little worried. I don't believe he's ill, but something was strange. He called me and couldn't remember why he called." She smiled. "That didn't surprise me. I do it all the time. But then he sounded strange, almost incoherent. I was worried he'd had a stroke, but then he began making sense." Rarity fiddled with her car keys. "Well, he told me he hadn't eaten breakfast, so that explained it. Low blood sugar. The man probably got busy working on one of his projects and forgot to take care of himself."

"That sounds like Wallace. With you delivering his lunch, he'll have to sit down and eat. If you want me too, I can look in on him later this afternoon."

"No. Don't go to any bother. I'm sure he'll be fine." She took a step toward the cash register and paused to look back. "Maybe you could stop in this evening. A casual visit. Don't let him know you're checking on him."

"No problem. I'll ask him to loan me a screwdriver or something. He's used to me borrowing tools."

Rarity collected her order and rushed out to climb into her VW bug.

Lines creased Anita's forehead. "How old is Wallace? Things happen to older people. Sometimes they ignore warning signs and put off going to a doctor. You should definitely stop in."

"He's one of the strongest men I know. Probably just forgot breakfast like Rarity said." I leaned back in the booth. "He behaves like he's forty but I'd guess he's in his late sixties. It would be just like him to forget to eat. He's fine."

Chapter Nine

I scoped out Wallace's house as I parked the Chrysler. His truck sat in its spot in the driveway. The grass looked recently mowed and trimmed. His windows were open to let in the breeze. Very peaceful and restful.

On the other hand, I could practically hear my computer calling me to get to work. I'd been spending too much time worrying about Evelynton's latest death and not enough about my writing. If an article didn't find its way to my editor soon, my bank account would be short when my bills were due. Maybe I'd wander next door, later, to check on Wallace. Borrowing a tool was always and good excuse and I really could use a wrench to fix a loose hinge on the kitchen cabinet.

Mason came at a gallop as I opened the front door. Crouching to receive a feline welcome, I almost had him in my arms before he reversed direction and dashed for the back door.

"What kind of greeting is that?"

My weird cat skidded to a stop in the kitchen, spun around and ran back to meet me in the dining room. I hadn't reached him when he turned tail and loped to the back door.

"Alright. Alright, I'm coming. What's so important?" I made it to the door and pushed it open, fearing he'd have a heart attack if he had to wait any longer. But instead of running for freedom, Mason sat still. He perched in the doorway with his eyes on the yard.

It was then that I saw the cause of the frenzy. "Oh my." Branches, leaves, and a fallen tree limb concealed much of my lawn. It wasn't so much a limb as half the tree. The old maple had hovered over the yard, providing shade in the summer and tons of leaves to rake in the fall, probably as long as the house had been there. Now a good part of it sprawled on the ground, reaching from one side of the yard to the other.

My knees went all wobbly, and I sank to the step next to Mason. "What happened? What am I going to do with it?"

As I considered my options, an old woman ambled down the alley. I'd seen her before in her daily walks around the block. She came to a halt at my property and scowled at me. Maybe she didn't actually scowl. It might have been her normal expression. "That's a mess."

No kidding? I hadn't noticed.

"You'll have to get that cleaned up."

Thanks for the wise advice.

"Yes, I sure will. It wasn't there when I left this morning. I guess it just happ—" The woman had turned away and continued her trek down the alley, so I shut my mouth and went back to considering options.

Number one, faithful option, Wallace. Thank goodness for the man who'd been available for advice since the day I'd moved in. He would know what to do, and he'd be happy to help.

I hopped over branches and ducked under tree limbs on my way to his back door. When tapping received no answer, I pressed my face to the screen and peered in. About five feet away, Wallace sat with his elbows on the kitchen table. To all appearances, he was contemplating empty burger-wrappings. "Yoo-hoo. Hello, Wallace."

He raised his chin and his eyes widened. "Hey, where did you come from? Sneaking up on me?" He waved me in. "Don't stand outside."

I stepped into his kitchen, thinking older people had earned the right to be a little strange. Maybe I'd caught him on the verge of a nap. "Sorry to barge in on you. Did you see what happened in my back yard?"

Wallace stood and joined me at the door to follow my pointing finger. "When did that get there? I didn't see it yesterday."

"Had to have fallen this morning while I was at work."

Wallace pushed through the door. "Let's take a look." Before we got off the steps, his wall phone jingled and he hustled back inside. "Hold on. Let me get this and I'll be over. We'll figure out what to do about that tree."

Sweet words. In the six years I'd been alone, being the one in charge of solving every problem had been a struggle.

"Wallace Binion, you're the best. Thank you so much." I left him to his call and picked my way through branches to my porch. Mason crawled onto my lap and I stroked his head. "Nothing to worry about. Wallace will take care of it."

I waited, watching leaves blow around the yard. I waited, and glanced at Wallace's back-door. I scratched Mason's ears. "Wonder who called? I've never known Wallace to be so talkative. Must have been Rarity. She could talk for hours."

The feline jumped from my lap and ran to play on the fallen limb. I sat another five minutes before making my way back across the yard to see what had happened to my neighbor. I peeked into the kitchen. The phone was back in its cradle. The table and chairs sat empty. A shout got no reply. A call to his cell phone went unanswered.

Leaving Wallace's back door, I made the trek around to the front of his house and found my answer. No truck in the driveway. He'd left without telling me.

I pivoted to return home and tripped over Mason. "It must have been an important call. Sure would've been nice if he'd have let me know he wasn't coming over." Mason uttered a tiny peep, spun and ran to the back-yard.

~~

Later that afternoon engine noise brought me to attention. Breathing a sigh, I scooped up Mason and went to the window. Wallace's truck was home. "Don't worry, Mason. He'll be over now."

I sat on the sofa with a magazine until the setting sun cast shadows across my living room. The street lights came on. Still no help from Wallace.

Disappointed, I gave up on my guardian neighbor, and stalked to the back porch to switch on the outside light. The scene hadn't changed. Mason trotted past me and climbed the fallen limb.

I wanted to scream. I stomped my foot, banged the screen door shut, and yelled at my poor cat. "You might think this is a jungle gym, but I have to get it cleaned up."

The cat crouched and appraised me with his round, golden eyes. "Sorry, it isn't your fault. I'm a grown woman. I can take care of it." I called the next person on my go-to list.

After I'd whined to Anita for ten minutes, she said, "I've got it. I have the number of someone who knows how to do everything. Do you remember all the odd jobs Jake never got around to doing for me a year ago? I found a handyman named Ted, who made quick work of them."

I stared out the window at the back yard where Mason performed flying leaps in his new play area. He swung from branch to branch, balanced, dropped to the ground and scurried up another limb.

"What's his number? I've already had a complaint, so I need him soon."

"The people on your block are all really nice, but let the tree lie there very long and someone will call City Hall. Since I know Ted, why don't I call and ask him to contact you? I'll tell him it's important. And I'll even loan him Jake's chainsaw if he needs it. That tree will be cleaned up before you know it."

Chapter Ten

Pounding on the front door set my heart pumping and sent my first cup of coffee to the floor. Once I caught my breath, I grabbed a paper towel and threw it over the puddle. While stomping to the door, I toggled through a mental list of possible visitors. No one, who knew me, would be crazy enough to arrive before nine. Except Clair, but I'd declined recent early morning power-walks.

I peeked through the window and found myself looking into sparkling green eyes. A chubby face smiled back at me. The massive man on my porch wore an olive work shirt, just a bit too small. The buttons strained across a belly that hung over matching work pants. His shaggy gray hair needed cut, and his last shave seemed to have been hit or miss.

Thinking about my uncombed hair and the sweats I'd worn as pajamas, I guessed I shouldn't be judgmental. I opened the door.

"Good morning, ma'am. I'm Ted the handyman. Mrs. Corbin sent me. She said you had some urgent work, so I came right away."

I forgot the spilled coffee and the uncivilized hour.

This was a good start to the day. "Thank you for coming so soon. Great service."

I stepped onto the porch. "Let's go around to the backyard and I'll show you the problem." While I led the way, I realized I'd seen him before. "Have we met? You look familiar."

"Yes ma'am, we have. I installed your phone and Internet hook-up about a year ago."

"Sure, I remember. You were one of the first people I met when I got to town." That man had been more acquainted with the razor and the barber. And that unkind observation reminded me of my own appearance. I raked my fingers through my hair. "Do you still work at the phone company?"

"No ma'am. I started my own handy man company. I do all kinds of work. Minor repairs, lawn mowing, leaf pick-up, snow removal. Sometimes I even wash windows. The wife calls me Jack-of-all-trades. But my name's Ted."

"Congratulations. I bet it's rewarding being your own boss. I hope this job is something you're interested in. About half a tree broke off and is lying in my yard."

We'd reached the backyard. Ted put his hands on his hips and scanned the debris. "I see you need a bit of clean-up. She's had a bad fall."

She?

"Would you be able to cut the limbs and haul them away? Do you think the whole tree needs to taken down?"

Ted leaned back, lifting his chin to study the tree from top to bottom. "Ah. The silver maple. She's a grand tree. Beautiful foliage. Her leaves shimmer like diamonds with the slightest breeze."

The man's a poet.

"Now that you mention it, I guess I have noticed the pretty leaves."

"Let's see if she's still strong." He stroked the tree with a gentle hand, then leaned his full weight on it. He stepped back and pounded on the trunk. "She's good and strong. Just needs trimmed and cleaned. Then we'll get her healthy again. You'll need to paint over the injuries right away so she doesn't bleed. Don't want her to get infected."

"A tree bleeds? It—she might get infected?" I had one more thing to feel guilty about. Caring for the cat had been a stretch for me. Now I was responsible for the health of a tree as well.

Ted eyed me for a moment, probably recognizing a clueless expression. "I'll bring a bucket of wound paint and take care of her."

We bargained about the price. Not so much bargained, as he told me what he wanted and I agreed. Ted promised to return the next day.

"I work in the morning, but will be home after lunch. If you'd prefer, you can wait until then to start. That way I can pay you as soon as you finish." I made a mental note to stop at the bank for cash.

"That won't be a problem. We want to get her fixed up as soon as possible. I'll be here first thing. If you aren't home by the time I'm finished, I can stop back."

"I'll give you my phone number. Just let me know if anything changes." I grabbed a sticky note from the house and handed it to Ted.

~~

Before leaving for work, I locked the door to the

back porch, blocking Mason's exit. "Don't glare at me. You'll be in Ted's way and might be injured. I'll let you out when I get home." The longer I lived with the cat, the more I felt the need to explain myself. He planted his feet and glared until I resorted to Aunt Ruth's answer for everything. "I'm the boss and I said so."

Mason curled up on the sofa and refused to acknowledge me as I left for work.

~~

I breathed a sigh and watched the Rare Curl clock strike twelve noon. Shift over, I ran for the Chrysler and took a direct route home, confident Ted would have taken care of the tree. One less problem on my plate. My driveway was empty, but I guessed his truck would be parked in the alley.

Tossing my handbag on the dining room table, I picked up Mason on my way through the kitchen. We stopped at the back door. The two of us gazed at a yard littered with tree limbs. Mason wriggled free and jumped to the floor, eager to play on the fallen tree. "I'm glad you're happy. I'm steamed. Doesn't look as if Ted was here at all." I stomped back inside.

What would Rarity say in this situation? I heard her sweet voice whisper, "Be patient. Practice grace. Something must have happened. Must have had to change his plans." My, not-so-sweet, voice butted in. "And he lost my number. Or his phone battery died so he couldn't call me."

I could be patient. I would follow Rarity's advice, as soon as I looked up the word grace in the dictionary. My good intentions prevailed through an entire five minutes spent pacing from the kitchen to the dining room and back. Then I phoned Anita. "Have you heard from Ted? He didn't show up today. I guess he decided he didn't want to do my job. Maybe found something better?"

"He wouldn't do that. Ted's very reliable. Maybe there was a misunderstanding. Are you sure he agreed to start today?"

"He said he'd be here 'first thing' and I took that to mean this morning. How else should I understand it? He could have at least let me know he wasn't coming. I counted on him. Even barricaded poor Mason in the house all morning."

Anita's voice was calm—even sweet. "I'm sure he had a good reason. I hope he isn't sick or injured. Maybe I should call and check on him."

Why did Anita always jump to the best conclusion about people, when I took giant leaps in the other direction?

"You're right. Something came up, or I misunderstood. Maybe he meant tomorrow. I'll skip coffee at Ava's in the morning, so I can be here when he arrives."

~~

With visions of Ted the handyman at my door bright and early, I showered and dressed before even brewing the coffee. No simple accomplishment for me. When he hadn't made an appearance by the time I'd finished breakfast, I attempted to work at the computer. That didn't work, because I couldn't stop myself from checking the drive every few minutes. Finally deciding it was another no-show for Ted, I managed to finish an article.

Early in the afternoon, while I prepared lunch, the

high-pitched whine of a chain saw disrupted the silent neighborhood. I carried my plate to the window. Ted was visible in the midst of a sawdust cloud. Woodchips flew as he leaned into the job.

Mason perched on the sill with his face to the window while I stood behind him munching a tomato sandwich, equally fascinated. At intervals, Ted dropped the saw and loaded logs into his pickup. Then he wiped his face with a handkerchief and went back to sawing. After twenty minutes, I left Mason to maintain the vigil, and returned to my work. I anticipated a pristine backyard by dinnertime.

Before long the cat wrapped himself around my feet. "Bored already? How's he doing?" Nudging my toes from under the feline, I slid out my chair and ventured to the porch. Piles of sawdust and cut logs lay scattered across the yard. No handyman in sight.

I pushed through the screen door and strolled to the alley. Ted and his truck were gone. I returned to the computer. The next time I pulled my attention from the screen, shadows of the setting sun spread across the room. I'd finished the article with no distractions. Mason climbed onto my lap to have his ears scratched. "Guess Ted had something else to do. What do you think? Will he finish tomorrow?"

~~

I'd become used to the idea of the disaster in the yard, and only glanced out the window twice while getting ready for work. I succeeded in locking the door to the porch before Mason made a dash for freedom. "Only one more morning. I'm sure he'll be here today to finish."

I was trotting to the Chrysler when Wallace

stepped out of his house. He waved. "I see you had some branches fall in the back."

I clamped my teeth together and fought the urge to ask him if he'd lost his mind. He was a busy man and had the right to forget some things. "Sure did. I think the handyman will finish clearing it today."

"That's good. Have a nice day at work." Wallace climbed into his truck and was out of his drive before I'd turned the ignition in my wagon.

Men.

After grumbling to myself for most of my four hour shift at The Rare Curl, I'd determined be at peace, and think about grace. I'd forget about the timber in my yard and undisciplined lumberjack. I'd enjoy lunch with my friends. Ava's Java would be a good distraction from such worries.

Anita pulled her handbag from the extra chair as I placed my salad on the table. "How's the tree situation?"

I concentrated on adjusting my utensils. "Ted's been working on it."

She grinned. "Aren't you amazed at how capable he is? I bet you've thought of a whole list of chores for him."

My jaw tightened. "I think I'll wait to see if he finishes this job. Haven't been impressed so far." Rarity's sage counsel about offering grace escaped me while I blurted out my frustrations of the last few days.

"I don't understand it. He was always right on time for me." Anita paused. "Last time he arrived just as I was pulling the chocolate chip cookies from the oven. Time before that, the cinnamon rolls hadn't even cooled."

Wait. What? "Cinnamon rolls? Cookies? And you fed Ted?"

"Of course. They smelled so good, I couldn't make the man suffer."

"You bake for him? That's why he was always on time?"

"Not every time. Once there was only left-over cherry pie."

Clair giggled. "The man works for snacks."

I closed my eyes and thought about banging my head on the table.

"Oh, no." Anita hesitated. "That can't be it." She stopped and crinkled her brow.

"I can't bake in the morning." Making coffee and pouring cereal into a bowl was an accomplishment. "Maybe I could pick up something at the Quik-mart."

Anita looked as if I'd uttered an obscenity. "I'm sure he'd prefer homemade. Probably gets enough store-bought at home. I think his wife works."

Clair cut in. "It isn't fair to ask Lauren to cook."

I cut my gaze to Clair and shifted it to Anita. "I can cook."

Anita gave me that sweet smile of hers. "I have lots of time. Why don't I bring something over next time?"

I let out a sigh and rearranged my salad on the plate. "Maybe I'll get some frozen cookie dough. I'll get up early and throw it in the oven."

~~

I stayed under the speed limit and set my mind on pleasant thoughts all the way home. When I reached Stoneybridge, Ted's blue pickup truck sat in the drive. Leaving my Chrysler on the street, I followed a trail of sawdust to the backyard. Ted gave me a courteous nod as he passed me with a wheelbarrow full of wood chunks and scraps. I reversed direction to watch him empty it into the bed of the truck.

"All finished?"

He dusted his hands on the green work pants. "Yes, ma'am. Soon as I mend the wound she'll be in fine shape." The big man hefted a ladder and a bucket from the truck bed, lugging them to the maimed tree. "This'll keep her healthy." He glanced at me as he climbed the ladder. "Did you know she symbolizes wisdom and unity? That's the Sugar Maple, but it's the same for the Silver."

"Didn't know that." I fled to the house wondering if I would need to provide the feminine, and wise, Silver Maple aspirin while she healed.

Twenty minutes later, Ted tapped at the front door. I paid him and he left. No baking required.

My cat rolled on the floor, playing with a tiny piece of wood. "Finally, things are getting back to normal around here, Mason."

Chapter Eleven

I breezed into The Rare Curl and glanced, out of habit, at the old clock on the wall. It read 4:15. That was to be expected. The hands, in the shape of scissors, hadn't budged in at least a month. The digital time on my cell phone read 8:00 a.m. Right on time by my standards, not my father's. His voice still echoed in my head. "If you roll in to work on the dot, you're fifteen minutes late. Arrive early enough to be alert and prepared to work when your shift begins." Heard by my fourteen-year-old self, not in any hurry to clerk at the grocery store, it hadn't seemed important. A number of years later, I began to see the wisdom. I usually invested ten minutes stashing personal items, adjusting my chair, and other actions meant to get me settled. Then, I'd spend another five minutes silently rehearsing professional answers to appointment requests. The years of working at home, alone, had taken a toll on my social skills.

Only one customer in the salon, so far. The fact that the woman was already parked in Rarity's chair with wet hair, shampoo cape, and coffee, indicated she'd arrived at least ten minutes earlier.

I stashed my handbag and called to her. "Good morning Gladys. You're here bright and early."

The long-time customer waved. "Yeah. They called me in to work this afternoon. Bless her heart, Rarity came in early, just for me."

A quick scan of the appointment book showed no other appointments for thirty minutes, giving me time to settle in. The squeak of the supply room door caused me to spin my chair to greet my employer. As I'd expected the petite salon owner stepped out, but she wasn't alone. A skyscraper of a woman dwarfed Rarity by at least eight inches. When they reached me, I tilted back, staring up at the newcomer. It would have been polite to stand, but I remained rooted to the chair.

Rarity placed her hand on her companion's arm and smiled at me. "Lauren, you'll be excited to hear we have a new stylist. This is Ellen Felicity. She joined us yesterday and got acquainted with the salon. Would you believe she's been passing out business cards, and already has some appointments? Isn't that great? Ellen's going to fit right in. And I know the two of you will get along wonderfully."

My brain was still busy calculating the height of the new employee. While my mind ticked away, I noticed Ellen Felicity had extended her hand. I jumped up to return the handshake. Unfortunately the action sent my chair rolling across the room. My "Nice to meet you." suffered under the crash of the chair spinning into the retail cabinet.

I winced at the racket. Rarity's eyes darted in the direction of the display case and back. "I'll leave you to get acquainted while I get started on Gladys's hair." She pulled a pair of shears from her pocket and joined her customer.

I tucked a loose hair into my ponytail and scanned Ellen Felicity's attire. Would she fit in? At The Rare Curl we tended to be lax in dress code, priding ourselves in dressing comfortably. Most days Rarity wore black slacks and a colorful top. Her natural curls ruled her hairstyle, never landing in the same spot two days in a row. Stacy loved leggings and wore them with a long shirt almost every day. In the last year she'd resorted to wearing sneakers because of a full work schedule. Her hairstyle changed daily, arranged in whatever style and color she'd found in the current magazines.

The new arrival wore high-heels and a short black skirt with matching fitted jacket. Her makeup was magazine perfect. The woman's shimmering blond, chin-length bob laid so perfectly I had a feeling not one strand of hair ever strayed from its position.

I ignored the over-turned chair, and followed Ellen Felicity's pointing finger. She hung over the appointment book, issuing orders. "I'll list precise timing for each service. And I ask that you always arrange a fifteen minute consultation for each new client. After the first appointment, you may schedule them for the normal time allotment afforded each service, unless I inform you differently."

My eyebrows began to scrunch together, and I thought it prudent to change the subject. "May I ask where you're from? You have an interesting accent that I can't place. Is it European?"

Ellen Felicity laughed. "I'm from right here in Evelynton, but don't tell anyone. I did some traveling after school. When I left home I practiced speaking with different accents. I eventually developed this one to set myself apart. It's British inflection with slight Italian overtones. I feel it's sophisticated without pointing to a specific nationality. Don't you agree?"

"Uh-huh. It does set you apart."

"I was determined to be a professional—not to clerk in a store or work as receptionist somewhere. Then it came to me. I returned to Indiana to attend cosmetology school. My fortune would be made by offering something special. I strive to be a step above other hairstylists in the area."

She picked up my notepad and found a pen in my drawer. "My first guest will be in soon. We should get back to the business at hand. Let me list a few reminders for you." With precise script she recorded each service along with the time allotted. "If you have questions, don't hesitate to ask. Of course I prefer you don't interrupt me while I'm working."

A vein throbbed above my left ear.

Ellen continued. "I understand you're rather casual about communication here, and it'll take time to get used to my way of doing things. But don't worry, I'll remind you. And I'll check every evening to make sure you've scheduled the next day appropriately."

My eyes blurred as I stood next to the desk watching her fill the notepad.

"Let me think. What else?" Ellen tapped herself on the head and strolled around the waiting area, carrying my notepad. I made and attempt to silence the groans each time she jotted an additional note. "Offer the guest coffee. Help the guest with her coat in cold weather." She finally produced what I considered a satisfied smile and strutted back to my side. I reached for the list and almost had it my possession, but she kept it locked in her grip. I tugged. She held firm. I looked her in the eye and pulled harder until she released the note pad into my care.

I sighed, thinking she'd finished torturing me, but her mind was still working. "One more thing. I'll welcome each guest at the reception desk. And would you please greet them as Mrs. Mr. or Miss, as the case may be? Shall I write that down? I am particular about how my clients are cared for."

"No need to list it. I'll remember, I promise."

"I hope so, dear."

Dear? I put my head back and studied the ceiling. *Rarity, what have you done?*

Fortunately, my boss and Gladys approached the desk before Ellen could think of one more thing to add. And before I gave in to the temptation to slap her.

I slid Gladys's check into the cash drawer hoping Ms. Felicity would go away. Instead her voice pierced my eardrum. "Bella! Your coiffure is simply bellissima."

Poor Gladys stared at Ellen as if she'd sprouted horns.

"Forgive me. Sometimes my grandmother's words of the old country come to mind before English. I meant your hair is beautiful. The perfect style for you."

Old country? Good grief.

I watched a pink tinge flow into Gladys's cheeks and a grin take over her face. The humble lady walked a little taller as she strutted from the salon. Ellen had won her over.

Rarity and Ellen left the reception area, and I used the time to retrieve my chair from the site of collision.

As I rolled it to the desk, Ellen marched to her styling station as if she owned the place. That area had been vacant for a year, since Patsy's arrest. Rarity had postponed filling the spot to allow all of us—customers and workers alike—to come to terms with the absence. We missed her. It's true she'd been homicidal, but she was one of ours. Patsy might have been easier to live with than Ellen promised to be.

Before my shift ended I managed to speak to Rarity privately. "Are you sure Ellen is the right fit for the salon? She seems to be particularly rigid in having things her own way."

Rarity slung her arm around my shoulders. "Don't you worry. I'm sure she'll grow on you as she gets used to the salon."

My boss tipped her head toward me and lowered her voice. "Ellen has had a rough time in the last couple of years. She's in need of cash, so she's determined to build her business. That will be good for us. Be patient with her."

"Sorry Rarity. I shouldn't jump to conclusions."

The truth was, I'd never been the best judge of character. Patsy turned out to be a murderer, yet I remembered her with fondness. Ellen Felicity may be hard to get along with, but at least I wouldn't find her in my house, with a gun.

Chapter Twelve

I shoved open the door of Ava's Java, expending a little more force than necessary. But as the aroma of fresh coffee swirled around me, my jaw relaxed and the tension in my neck released. Standing just inside the door, I took a moment to inhale the scent of freshly ground beans. "Thank you, Lord, for coffee. And for friends." After picking up my cup from Ava, I found Anita and Clair seated at our favorite table.

Clair scooted her chair to the side to make room for me. "How was your day at work?"

I shut my eyes for a second, taking time to construct a kind answer. Unfortunately, a sharp retort found its way out. "Fine."

Guess I shouldn't have revisited the thoughts of the day. Neck muscles twitched and twisted. I gazed at Clair and spat the words out. "It was terrible. There's a new hairdresser at The Rare Curl, and I don't like her." There I'd said it. My friend's eyes widened. I rushed ahead. "Rarity thinks she's wonderful, but she's bossy and snobbish. Doesn't fit in at all. The dynamics of the place are already changing. It won't be comfortable anymore."

Anita emptied a packet of sugar into her cup. "Blond? Really tall? Looks like a model?"

I nodded. "That's her."

"I saw her going into the salon yesterday. She's very glamorous."

"That's another thing. The way she dresses makes the rest of us look like we're working a garage sale. I felt like a bag lady."

"You always look nice." Anita put a hand on my arm. "Rarity's usually a good judge of character. I bet you'll find she's right about this employee."

I wasn't ready to listen. "Did I say the woman is bossy? Tried to tell me how to do my job. I know how to be a receptionist. I'm good at it."

Clair set down her coffee. "Wow. Listen to you. I've never heard you say you didn't like anyone. You might suspect them of murder, but you've never expressed dislike."

Anita gave me the look that reminded me of the town librarian. "We all have pointy corners to our personalities. Some sharper than others. You're seeing hers now. As you work together for a common cause—the salon—the prickly parts get smoothed over. You'll get used to her. Is this the first day you've worked with her?"

I hung my head, feeling like a scolded child. "I only met her four hours ago. Guess I overreacted. I could give it some more time. I'm sure I'll become accustomed to her eccentricities—eventually."

"Great. I knew you'd figure it out. Glad you're feeling better." Clair sat up straighter and wrapped long fingers around her coffee mug. "On a more interesting note, I wonder how long it will take the police to release the dead woman's house so it can be sold."

Anita stirred more sugar into her coffee. "What do you suppose happened to that poor woman? Ava told me people are betting she had an aneurysm or something."

"I doubt even the forensics people could tell after so much time has elapsed. I wish they'd get on with it." Clair tapped a bright red fingernail on the table. "Just goes to show, you never know when your time on earth is up. Better keep your affairs in order." She stared into Anita's eyes. "You and Jake have made your wills haven't you?"

"Oh sure, long ago. We had to provide for the girls in case something happened to us." Anita glanced in my direction. "Have you made arrangements?"

"No. Why would I need arrangements? What do I have to leave anybody? And who would I leave it to? Tell you what, I'll take care of it right now." I faced Anita. "If something happens to me, will you take care of Mason?"

Anita's face softened. "Awww. Of course. I love that furry little guy. Thank you for trusting me with him."

She straightened up and squinted at me. "Hold on a minute. We're not talking about right now. You're not going to drop dead tomorrow. God willing, it will be many years. But this is serious. You own a house and you will still own a car. Probably not the one you drive now, of course."

My Chrysler station wagon was thirty-five years old when my aunt left it to me last year. I couldn't imagine how she'd kept it running as long as she had, but it was still carrying me. "Let's hope I'll be changing transportation soon."

"Are you sure you don't want the SUV we found in the mummy woman's house? You could probably get it for free." Clair grinned at me over the top of her coffee.

I shuddered and threw a napkin at her. "Ugh. You have a strange sense of humor, Clair Lane."

Anita glanced over my shoulder toward the counter. "Look. There's Perry. Haven't seen him in here for a while."

Clair and I twisted to follow her gaze. Our former classmate was making his way to us. Never a small person, he'd seen considerable weight gain in the years since graduation. Perry maneuvered his girth through the crowded coffee shop until he'd arrived at our table.

Clair leaned back and lifted her chin. "Perry Sizemore, how are you? Where have you been hiding?"

"Hello beautiful." His eyes swept the table, eyes lingering on each of us. "I should say, hello all you gorgeous ladies. I'm speechless in the presence of the three most attractive women in town."

Anita pointed at him. "You've never been speechless in your life."

Perry's laugh echoed in the room.

"Jake and I've missed seeing you since he hasn't been able to play this summer."

Perry touched Anita's hand. "I've missed our golf dates. I hope his ankle is on the mend."

"He's determined to be on the course again by spring."

"Good to hear. Good to hear." He reached back and pulled a chair from a nearby table. "May I join you? I haven't had the pleasure of conversation with such lovely ladies in a while."

I guess he didn't expect a negative response, since he'd lowered himself into the chair and begun the process of scooting it closer. With one last scoot his ample belly bumped the table, sloshing coffee.

Clair and I snatched up our cups to keep them from tipping. Anita grabbed a napkin to mop up spilled liquid while she scanned the area around him. "Do you have enough room there?"

He stretched to place his coffee within reach at the edge of the table. "Perfect. I'm the envy of every man in the room."

My friends and I wore matching polite smiles as Perry arranged himself in the seat. I imagined they wondered, as I did, when he'd run out of the corny flirtations.

He tipped his head toward Clair and lowered his voice. "There's talk around the office you got a big surprise when you went to assess a property. I bet that was one time you wished my firm got the contract instead."

Clair set her mug on the table. "I wouldn't wish that on you, even though you are my biggest competitor."

The large man made an effort to lean back in his chair, but had already filled the space. "It was a tragedy. Have the police said anything to you about how Valentina died?"

Our three heads pivoted in his direction, all eyes focused on him. Clair spoke. "Valentina? Was that her name? How did you know her?"

Perry stretched forward to get his cup, took a slow sip of coffee, and he set it back in its place while we waited. "Valentina Utkin. I met her about a year ago, at the club. The guys and I went in for a drink after a round of golf. She was sitting by herself, so I started a conversation—just to be friendly. Hate to see anyone sitting alone."

Clair slid her chair closer to the table, staring into Perry's eyes. "Tell us about it."

Perry, who couldn't resist being the center of attention, lowered his voice. "As you know I'm always on the look-out for leads, so pretty soon I was telling her about the housing market. Let her know if she ever wanted to sell, the time was right."

Anita leaned in. "Was she interested in selling? Did you see her house? What age would you say she was? What was she like? Did she say what she did for a living?"

Perry's mouth hung open until she'd finished rattling off questions. "Umm, I suppose she was in her thirties. Or maybe early forties? Nice looking. I could tell she took care of herself, like you girls. But as I said, I only met her that one time, and it was casual. Not personal at all."

He took another swig of coffee. "I saw her house—the outside of it. She'd given me directions so I could do a drive by. That's what grabbed my attention when it was on the news. I remembered the address because it's my job. Anyway, I called after I checked it out and gave her a ball-park figure." He waved a hand. "She wasn't interested, so I let it drop. But that was a year ago. Maybe more. I'm surprised the address stuck with me."

Clair hadn't missed a syllable. "So you talked to her twice?"

Perry shook his head. "No." Then his eyes widened. "Oh, I guess I did."

I'd never been comfortable with Perry, even on his best behavior, which I hadn't seen since my return to Evelynton. He was more flirtatious than I thought a married man should be. So at this moment I was torn between wanting him to go away, and the niggling need for more information. "Utkin's an interesting name. Was she from Europe? Did she speak with an accent?"

Perry tipped his head back and guffawed. "Did she have an accent! And sexy. She could've stepped right out of a Bond film. I expected her to pull a revolver from her garter." He leaned forward and produced a sly smile. "I have to say she wouldn't have needed one. I'd have gone anywhere with her." Perry's smile faded fast and he began to sputter. "She sounded Russian to me but what do I know? I didn't ask her nationality. Like I said, we only spoke for a few minutes, and it was mostly business."

Anita was insistent. "What did the woman do for a living? Did she say?"

"No. She never said." Perry shook his head and scooted his chair out. "I hate to leave you ladies but this is a work day and my schedule calls. Have a great afternoon." He left his cup on the table and his chair in the middle of the aisle, as he made a break for the door."

Anita scooted forward, whispering. "This is exciting. A Russian woman found dead in Evelynton, Indiana." She flicked her hair back from her face and tried on a Russian accent. "Hello darling, my name is Valentina Utkin."

Clair and I laughed, but Anita sobered quickly.

"Sorry. The poor woman is dead."

"You're right. How insensitive of us." I wondered about Valentina Utkin. Who had she been? "How could a woman live in that house without anyone knowing her, and then die with no one being aware? Didn't she have anyone who cared enough to notice she was missing?"

We sat in silence for a few minutes while my brain went into overdrive sorting through scenarios. I slapped the table. "I bet this is what happened. We've concluded she lived alone and didn't have any friends, at least not in Evelynton. She was far from her homeland. Probably from Russia or Kazakhstan."

Anita faced me. "Where's Kazakhstan?"

"I have no idea. But it's a great name, don't you think? Anyway, maybe Valentina was from some obscure country and in hiding. She'd fled her homeland because of political persecution. Couldn't return. Never to see her family again. Then, she became so lonely and depressed she killed herself." I took a deep breath. "Or the foreign government tracked her down. They crept into town one night, assassinated her, put her body in the car so she wouldn't be found, and sneaked out of Evelynton the same day. No one the wiser."

Clair cut her eyes to me. "You're constructing quite a tale, Mystery Woman."

I slapped my hand over my mouth as I returned to reality. "Oh. I guess I was embellishing a little. But it could fit the facts."

Clair had given me the nickname Mystery Woman during my first month back in Evelynton. She told me I found mysteries behind every door and new questions around every corner.

But really, didn't everyone?

I wasn't ready to let the subject drop. "Did you believe Perry? Do you think he only met the Utkin woman the one time? I thought he emphasized that point more than necessary. Maybe there was more to the relationship than he wants known."

Clair slurped her coffee. "Once you get started, that mystery seeking brain of yours can't stop."

Anita leaned forward and grabbed my wrist. "I agree with you. There is more to the story, and I'd love to find out what it is."

She paused. When I didn't respond, she went on. "You said all Valentina's belongings were in the house. Don't you wish we could search her things? There are bound to be clues to her life. Let's try to get in. Valentina's house looks just like Tonya's, so it probably has a sliding door in back. They're easy to open."

Had I created a monster?

I shook my head. "Don't even think about it. That would probably be against the law. You are aware that I can't afford another conflict with Jimmy Farlow, right?"

Anita's eyes had taken on a wicked gleam. "Come on, we'll only take a little look. I know the people who live behind the dead woman's house—Jean and Jerry Parker. They're out of town for a month. We could leave the car in their drive and cut through the backyard." She leaned back and grinned. "It'll be easy."

She glanced toward Clair. "It would be easier if you still had the keys. Do you?"

Clair threw up her hands. "You're both crazy. No! I gave both sets to the police."

"Darn. But I know how to get in."

"You do? How?" I paused to consider it. "No, I don't care how. It's a bad idea." My reply wasn't particularly convincing. I waited for her to persuade me.

Anita was whispering now. "We'll go in through the back yard at night."

Clair shifted in her chair to gaze at Anita. "You have lost your mind. What happened to the nice housewife I used to hang around with?" Her head swiveled toward me. "You aren't going to do it are you?"

I shook my head. "Absolutely not. We won't be breaking in to that house. Much too dangerous. No way."

Chapter Thirteen

Headlights lit up my living room window at exactly nine-thirty. I opened the door and shouldn't have been surprised that Anita had worn black pants and sweatshirt, almost identical to the outfit I'd chosen. She wore a navy bandanna to cover her blond curls. I'd pulled my hair into a ponytail.

Jeez. Twin cat burglars.

Anita's eyes flashed as she bounced into the entry. "All set? I brought two flashlights and Jake's flathead screwdriver to jimmy the door. Too bad we don't have night vision goggles."

I laughed. "That would be a bit over-the-top, don't you think?" I paused, letting the image sink in. "Do you think those are available on the Net? I wonder how much they would cost."

Anita drove. We'd realized, in a previous caper, that my thirty-five-year-old Chrysler station wagon was easily recognizable since it was probably the only one still on the road in all of Indiana—or anywhere.

Anita extinguished her headlights as we rolled into the Parker's driveway. As she'd predicted, the house was dark. We stepped out and closed the car doors as quietly as possible. Only two faint clicks were heard.

"This way." She whispered.

I followed Anita's shadow around the side of the house, too scared to use my flashlight until necessary. Out of range of streetlights, and with no moon to illuminate the way, I became disoriented and grabbed the back of her sweatshirt to steady myself. I kept my hand on Anita's back as we traversed the yard. We were stopped at a thick hedge, and had to crawl through on hands and knees. I made it through to Utkin's property with minor scratches and muddy knees.

Anita flicked on her flashlight and aimed it to the ground ahead of us as she picked up the pace. I tagged along, keeping close behind.

A dog barked in the next yard. I jumped and stifled a scream when a door opened at that house. Both Anita and I hit the ground, holding our breath until the dog was called inside and the door closed.

We breathed a joint sigh of relief, and got to our feet. Crouching low, we made our way to Utkin's sliding patio door.

I grabbed the handle. Locked. "Shoot. Now how do we get in?"

"Hold on, I got this." A low rumble sounded in the distance and a glimmer of lightning illuminated Anita digging into her pocket. Her hand came out with the screwdriver. She shoved her flashlight into my hand, hissing, "Shine it on the lock."

Raindrops began to fall, and I hunched my shoulders against the chill. The beam of the flashlight wavered in my trembling hand. But my friend seemed calm as she fiddled with the latch. A loud click sounded when the mechanism popped open.

My jaw dropped. "How did you know how to do that?"

She slid the door open and whispered. "I had brothers. I made them show me how to do stuff in return for not tattling to Mom about their escapades."

We stepped inside and gently pulled the door closed. Then reality struck. This was a break-in. My feet became anchored to the floor. My legs wouldn't respond to commands. Why had I returned to the house where I'd found a corpse? What if a murderer lurked in the shadows? Even worse, were the police watching the house? I twisted to look longingly through the glass door. Should we run back through the yard to the minivan?

Anita had moved on. "Let's go."

I took deep breaths to calm the erratic beating of my heart. After a minute I found I could edge one foot forward, and then the next.

My friend seemed to have no problem moving. The pool of light from her flashlight moved toward the bedrooms, so I followed. Her whisper came in the dark. "Turn on your flashlight. No one will see it. Just keep it aimed low so it won't show through the windows."

When did she become so savvy at sleuthing? And how long had I been such a coward?

"You've been reading detective novels haven't you?"

"Uh-huh."

"I thought you liked romance."

"Mystery's my new thing."

Anita turned left, off the hallway. I turned to the right, into a room I remembered as the master bedroom.

That was the room likely to hold the clues, if there were any to be found."

Thunder rumbled outside as I moved to the dresser and pulled out the bottom drawer. If I had anything to hide, I'd put it there. Not in the upper drawers where it would be disturbed while I was getting dressed every day. The drawer was filled with folded slacks and sweat pants. I slid my hand underneath. Nothing. That was disappointing. I glanced around the dark room and chills ran up my spine. Common sense told me we should get out before someone discovered us.

The wise side of my personality told me to call Anita, and to tell her this was crazy, we should leave. The other side of that fickle personality remembered she'd been so excited. How could I make her give up after only a few minutes? We were in the house. Had already committed the crime. I returned to the drawer, pulling out the slacks one at a time. Half way through the stack, I found it.

A book lay hidden between the layers. My breath came a little faster. This would be the clue we'd hoped for. I sat on the floor with the book on my lap and began turning pages. It was a scrapbook, but nothing like I'd expected.

Anita's spot of light entered the room. "There wasn't anything over there. How are you doing?"

I tried not to sound as giddy as I felt. "This photo album was in the drawer. She had hidden it in the middle of the clothes."

Anita directed her light at the book. "Are there pictures of her family? Any names?"

"No names that I've found. And I don't think these are family photos. It looks like Valentina did a lot of dating. At least I assume this is her. Hard to be sure, since this woman is healthy. I didn't see her body, but from Clair's description—"

"Stop. I don't need to hear the description again."

"Right."

I concentrated on the album. Each photo featured an attractive dark-haired woman snuggled up to a man. In almost every photo she wore formal attire. Her long hair was pulled into a severe chignon in some pictures and lay loosely on her bare shoulders in others. Low-cut gowns revealed ample cleavage.

"It's the same woman, but a different man in every snapshot. They all seem to be very friendly. These were definitely not business lunches. If this is Valentina, we needn't have worried about her being lonely. She seems to have had an active social life."

Anita lowered herself to the floor beside me and took over paging through the book. "Can't say she didn't enjoy life. There's one of her on the beach. Her bathing suit doesn't leave much to the imagination, does it?" She flipped to another page and moved her light closer. "Uh-oh. Look at that one."

I caught my breath. "It sure looks like Perry." Our classmate and the woman were seated close enough together to confirm they were more than casual acquaintances. The table in front of them was covered with a white table cloth and set with fine china plates filled with food. They held crystal wine glasses.

"It doesn't look like they're discussing the housing market. Do you recognize the restaurant? Way too fancy for anyplace in Evelynton."

"No, definitely out of town." Anita tapped her flashlight on Perry's picture. "Well, that big liar. It's obvious he knew Valentina Utkin much better than he said. They're on a date, and he's a married man. Shame on him."

I leaned back against the bed and let my flashlight lay on the floor. "That's discouraging. I'd like to think marriages were secure in this quiet little town, even for a flirt like Perry. I guess not."

"Now we know why he suddenly remembered he had to go to work, when we questioned him about Valentina." Anita twisted toward me. "You don't think he had anything to do with her death?"

"Not Perry. He's sort of creepy, but I can't believe he's a killer. There's something else going on here. How could she date so many different men? Why would she keep all their photographs? It looks like a trophy case."

My friend flicked off her flashlight. "That's what it is. She was a serial dater. Addicted to love. And if she fooled around with this many men, someone had a motive for murder."

The room lit up with a flash of lightning, followed by a clash of thunder. Then everything went dark again. All we heard was the sound of rain beating on the roof.

I turned my head toward Anita but could only see her eyes glistening in the dark. "Wait, we don't know that she was murdered. It could have been a natural death or suicide."

"You're right. Dating all these men would certainly have given me a heart attack." Anita switched on her light, directed it to the book, and turned the page. "Oh, he's cute."

"Hmm. He looks sort of familiar. Do you know him?"

"No, but he looks like someone famous. Probably has one of those faces that always looks familiar."

I flipped through a few more pages. "There must be a couple hundred photographs. It's a book filled with this woman's dating life." I slammed it shut. "The police need to see it. Let's put it back where I found it and let them discover it. We can't let on we were here."

"They've already been through the house. What if they're finished? How are we going to get them to find it?" Anita paused for a moment. "Maybe you can tell them you saw it in a dream."

"Right. I'm sure they'd run right over. They already think I'm a nut-case."

"I know. That's why I thought of it." She stifled a giggle.

Rumbling continued outside. I glanced at Anita. Short flashes of lightning illuminated the room enough to see her face for a few seconds each time. "I don't even want this book in my possession. You know if Officer Farlow had his way I'd be in jail."

"That's true. What are we going to do?"

"I don't know. We can't walk in and tell them we know there is a photo album in the dead woman's dresser. And 'No sir, we didn't break in, we just had a feeling.'"

The thunder grew louder.

The light from Anita's flashlight left the book. I twisted to see what she was doing and was met with a monstrous face with dark, elongated features. I swallowed a scream before I noticed my friend had aimed the light upward under her chin. The shadows transformed her pleasant face into something no one would want to see on a dark night.

"You nearly scared me to death." I flashed my light around the room. "This place is spooky. Let's put this book back where I found it and get out of here."

Anita kept her light shining under her chin and stuck out her tongue. "Let's take it and shove it into a mailbox, addressed to the police. That way they wouldn't be able to connect us to it."

"That's an idea, but the book's too big for a mailbox." I replaced half the clothing, placed the photo album on top, and covered it with the remaining clothes. After giving the drawer a firm push, I stood up. "Let's go. We can talk when we're safely back in the car."

I led the way down the hallway and through the living room. We pushed the sliding door shut and Anita stuck the screwdriver into the lock once again. The lock clicked.

"How did you do that? Never mind. I don't want to know."

The rain pelted us as we made our way through the yard. Clumps of my hair came loose from the ponytail and clung to my face. Water dripped from my nose and chin. I kept the flash-light pointed to the ground and picked up speed, trotting until I had to stop at the hedge. Anita, who'd been following close behind, slammed into my back propelling both of us into the bushes.

She erupted into giggles. "Wish we had a video of this. It would be hilarious."

"Shush!"

As I picked my way through the branches Anita grabbed my sleeve. "Do you think any of these homes have security cameras?"

Crap.

I froze and peeked out from the middle of the hedge. Wiping my hand over my face to clear the rain from my eyes, "Hard to tell. I can barely see the houses. Just keep the light to the ground and let's get out of here." We ducked our heads and ran for the minivan.

I slammed the door. "Turn on the heat. My teeth are chattering and there isn't a dry spot on my body."

"As soon as the motor warms up." Anita turned on the ignition, backed out of the drive, and started down the street. We'd barely traveled half a block before she slammed on the brake, sending me against the dash. "Poor Marlene. I hate the thought of her hearing about Perry's indiscretion from the police. Or worse, the newspaper. We should have confiscated that picture. Let's go back and get it." She shifted into reverse and twisted in her seat, to back up.

"Stop!" I grabbed the wheel. "We can't do that. For one thing, it would be tampering with the evidence—more than we already have. Second, do you want to leave a trail of wet footprints all the way through the house?"

Anita gazed down at the puddle around her feet. "You're right. We can't do it now. Wish I'd thought about it sooner."

She shifted into drive again. "I'll dry off and come back when the rain stops."

"Don't even think about it. It's too late. Promise me you won't break into that house again."

"Okay."

"I didn't detect real agreement in that answer. Promise."

"Alright, I promise I won't go back into the house."

"Good. Let's go home."

Anita was quiet as she drove—probably thinking of ways to get out of her promise.

I considered methods to reveal the new evidence without running the risk of prison time.

Chapter Fourteen

I splashed up the steps and pushed the front door open, pausing to catch my breath while rain water settled around my feet. Mason pussyfooted toward me, finally sitting back on his haunches to give me a reproachful stare.

"I can't help it. It's pouring outside."

I slid out of my shoes and ran for the bedroom, where I stripped off the soggy clothes. The first thing I found in my closet, that was dry and warm, was my oldest set of baggy sweats. Also, my favorite for sitting around the house. They weren't particularly attractive, but couldn't be more cozy.

On my way to the kitchen, I grabbed a towel and scrubbed at my hair to blot the moisture. After depositing the wet towel into the laundry basket, I searched the pantry for something to warm my frigid insides. I kept a box of cocoa on the shelf for just such occasions.

Mason sat at my feet and glared while I waited for the milk to steam, so I stooped to look him in the eyes. "Alright, what I did tonight probably wasn't my best idea. Not even close. We could have been caught. But I don't think anyone saw us, and we found some interesting information. Very likely evidence that could lead to the person who killed Valentina Utkin. If only I could figure out how to give it to the police without telling them how I found it."

The milk was hot so I stood and stirred in the cocoa. A rapping at the door caused both of us to jump. Mason recovered quickly, and pranced toward the door with his tail held high.

"Wait, I don't know if I want to answer it. Who could it be on a night like this?" Mason turned his eyes to me and purred. "So it's someone you like? Anita must have come back to help me decide what to do with the new information. Or to convince me to go back for Perry's picture, which is out of the question."

I reached the door and pulled it open without bothering to check the window. "Guess I should have made more hot chocolate."

Oops. I stood face-to-face with Jack Spencer, the man Clair still called Mr. Tall Dark and Handsome—with good reason. We'd had an on and off dating relationship. More off than on, since he lived two hours away.

An image of my towel blotted, but uncombed, hair flashed through my mind. *Oh crap.* "Jack. Um, hi. Come in. I didn't know you were in town." I stepped back to let him pass, waiting until his back was turned to rake my fingers through my hair.

"Hey. Sorry it's so late. I should've given you a heads-up, but this was last minute."

I'd always been a sucker for a deep manly voice, and his warmed my heart faster than any hot chocolate could. That's what I was thinking while Jack waited for a response. Receiving none, he continued. "I'm in town for a quick visit with Wallace and have to get back to the city right away, but I didn't want to leave without at least saying hello."

It dawned that I would have to say something to the man. "I'm glad you did. You're welcome to stop by anytime. I'm always happy to see you."

And as soon as you walk out the door, I promise I'm burning these ugly sweats.

Jack stood in the living room with his hands in his pockets. "I'm sorry for barging in. Did I interrupt your shower?"

I ran my hand through my hair. "Oh, no. I got caught in the rain. Anita and I were... Um, not important. I just got home."

Suddenly remembering the mug of cocoa in my other hand. "Isn't this the perfect night for hot chocolate? Would you like a cup? All the ingredients are out, so all I have to do is warm the milk."

"Thanks. That sounds good, but I have to be on the road. I had a case in the next county and talked to Wallace on the phone. He sounded under the weather, so I swung over to see him. He seems fine now."

"Has he been sick? I didn't know."

"I guess not. He says he's been fine. My mistake. But while I was here I wanted to tell you how much I enjoyed our dinner. I meant to call sooner. Time got away from me. What's it been? A couple of weeks?"

Four. It's been four weeks.

"Has it been that long? I didn't realize."

Jack continued. "You must think I'm a jerk. The fact is, getting my consulting business up and running has been more time-consuming than I expected."

"I understand completely. It must require all your time. And I never thought of you as a jerk."

The thought might have crossed my mind. But only once.

"With this new business, I don't have the time to devote to anyone, even someone as special as you are. You deserve better. But I'd like to remain friends."

"Of course. I'm not ready for a serious relationship either. Still trying to get my life together after moving back to Evelynton."

Water dripped off my nose, and I slapped at a drop trickling down my neck.

Smile lines crinkled at the corners of Jack's chocolate brown eyes. "I won't keep you. Better let you get back to drying off before you catch cold."

He took a step past me and grabbed the door knob. "I'll talk to you soon."

I wiped drops from my face. "Have a safe trip back to the city. Stop by anytime."

Before I knew it, he'd jogged across the lawn to his car.

I whispered, "Good night." and closed the door.

Back in the bathroom for another towel, I caught sight of my reflection in the mirror. It looked like I'd smeared charcoal under my eyes. "Yikes. Cat, why did you let me answer the door? You led me to believe it was safe."

I directed Mason's attention to the mirror, and demanded, "Look at me, I'm a mess. It's quite obvious I'm not ready for a serious relationship. Can't even receive an unexpected guest with dignity."

With the towel wrapped firmly around my head, I

plopped onto the sofa with my now lukewarm mug of cocoa. Mason took possession of my lap, curled up, and was soon drifting off to sleep. Living alone—with my cat—wasn't a bad thing. At least I didn't have to worry about my appearance all the time. And I liked my comfy sweats.

I lifted the feline's chin. "So back to less disturbing matters, Mason. What do you think? Charge into the police station and tell them what we discovered? Even at the risk of running into Jimmy Farlow? Or should I send an anonymous note?" Mason's tail swished until it landed across his face. "Is that your answer? Very wise. I should remain anonymous."

Light flashed outside. A moment later the windows rattled at a crack of thunder. "Another storm coming in." I flicked on the television, and rain began to pelt the glass.

Chapter Fifteen

Rarity loved the new clock she'd installed on the wall above the retail shelves. We'd agreed the oversized vintage timepiece was a lovely addition to our homey village salon. She'd mounted it, and then left to drive to the supply store. I sat at the desk waiting for the phone to ring, while the clock became increasingly intrusive. It punctuated the seconds, minutes and hours with incessant ticking. The noise tended to echo in the empty room.

Business was slow, more like non-existent, at The Rare Curl. Stacy wouldn't arrive until later for her afternoon schedule. No chattering customers sat in the waiting room. Ellen Felicity was on duty waiting for a possible walk-in, but we didn't talk. She'd swept and re-swept the floor around her styling chair. Eventually satisfied with its cleanliness, she'd taken a cloth to her mirror and counter-top. Vigorous scrubbing and polishing produced a high shine on the old surface. I wondered how that was possible.

I told myself it would be a nice gesture to compliment her, but my obstinate nature refused. The encouraging words wouldn't come out. In my defense, I'd already made several stabs at conversation. Each effort had won a single word answer, or a hum. So I'd washed and filled the coffee pot and completed all appointment reminder calls. Now, I sat at my desk, waiting and watching the second hand make its hesitant trip around the new clock.

A piercing jingle from the string of bells, attached to the front door, nearly startled me out of my chair. My gaze darted to the entrance with anticipation. Would it be the health inspector? Someone looking for the hardware store? Maybe a bank robber? Anyone would be a welcome intrusion.

My friend Anita held the door open and leaned in. "Are you busy? I'll go on to Ava's if I'm interrupting."

"No! Please don't leave. The only thing you're interrupting is my slow death from boredom. No customers this morning and the phone hasn't rung in an hour. What's up?"

She grabbed a chair on her way through to waiting room and dragged it close to the desk. "I got to town early for an appointment and wanted to talk to you about our little discovery last night." She fake whispered the last part.

"The photo album?"

"Yes. I couldn't sleep all night for wondering why Valentina Utkin kept all those pictures. And how could one woman have so many dates with different men? Who were they? And I still worry about that one picture." Lowering her voice to a fake whisper again. "The one of the man we know."

"It's too bad his photo's in the book, but I don't know what we can do about it. We can't take it out—

it's evidence."

Anita groaned. "I wish we hadn't left it there. With so many other photos of men, what does just one matter?"

"If the woman was murdered, the book is crucial. All of it. We can't go destroying evidence just because we happen to know one of the men she was involved with. If the alliance comes out, he'll face the consequences."

Furrows formed across Anita's brow, and I thought she might be close to tears. "I'm so worried."

"Have a cup of coffee."

"No thanks. I'm fine. I just want people to be happy."

"This whole case is so frustrating. I wish it were over." I also wished I hadn't let Anita talk me into breaking into the house. Looking for clues was fun. But the problem with discovering evidence was—it called for a response. "I'm sure they'll conclude Valentina committed suicide or had a heart attack. It'll be over, as far as our police department is concerned. They'll file the paperwork away. Even if they look through the book and recognize the picture, they won't have any reason to tell his wife."

"Okay. I know you're right. I agree we have to turn it over to the police. How are you going to do it?"

I leveled my eyes at Anita. "Me?"

Her eyes widened. "Well, you're good at that sort of thing."

"You mean I have a knack for blundering into police business and getting myself into trouble. But you're right, it should be me. There's no reason for you to be involved. You should be free in case I need you to post bail."

Anita gasped and wrinkled her brow.

I laughed but I'm not sure Anita bought it. She knew I was concerned. "Don't worry. I'll find a way to do this without telling them we broke into the Utkin's house."

"If we wait long enough, they'll rule on the cause of death. Maybe the pictures won't make any difference. We could forget all about it."

"True. How long do you suppose we can wait?" I massaged my temples while I thought about the tactic. "No. I don't feel good about withholding the information."

"You're right of course. The proper thing to do would be to give it to them." Anita paused to squint at me. "But don't do anything rash. Maybe there's a better plan." She raised her eyes to the ticking clock. "I have to get to my appointment. Now I'm late." She stood and returned her chair to the waiting area. At the door she said, "Consider alternatives, and we'll talk later."

Anita waved and scooted out to join the rush hour crowd on the sidewalk."

I pulled my chair closer to the reception desk and glanced at Rarity's clock. Still ten minutes before my boss would return. I doodled a hanging stick figure on the appointment book and wondered what the charge would be for entering Valentina Utkin's house, a possible crime scene, without permission. And even worse, would I be implicated in her murder—if it was murder?

The jingling front door brought me out of my bleak thoughts of life behind bars. Rarity and Stacy walked in together, breathing life into the suffocating salon.

Suddenly The Rare Curl was filled with chatter and activity.

The door to the stockroom squawked as Rarity carried in a bag of supplies, and once again as she exited the room followed by Ellen Felicity.

Rarity beamed. "Someone has been working hard. That supply room positively shines."

Ellen raised a shoulder. "I'm afraid I'm the guilty party. I took it upon myself to clean it. It looked as if it hadn't been cleaned in a while."

She gathered her handbag from the cabinet and breezed past me on her way to the front door. "I'm getting a cup of coffee."

I pointed to our coffee bar. "There's a full pot here."

The bells clattered against the door as it banged shut.

There was little time to wonder about my reclusive coworker. Women filtered in to fill the styling chairs and began shouting over the whine of blow-dryers. The phone, once it had broken its silence, didn't stop ringing.

Ellen Felicity returned, sipping her Blue Mountain Arabica coffee from a to-go cup, and took my position at the desk. My shift was over.

With my handbag slung over my shoulder I trotted to the car, determined to drive past the dead woman's house, one more time. She'd been on my mind since Anita's visit. Valentina was someone's daughter, maybe someone's sister. Was she a mother? From the looks of the scrapbook, she'd had many male acquaintances. How could she have lain secretly entombed in the garage for so long?

Chapter Sixteen

I drove into the quiet neighborhood and eased up on the accelerator, letting the Chrysler coast past Valentina Utkin's house. What would I see that I hadn't detected before? Was there something about the shrubbery or the exterior of the house that would provide insight into Valentina's life? Silly thoughts. This wasn't a detective novel where clues jumped out at the hero, and I don't believe murders return to the scene of the crime.

Sliding my foot back onto the gas pedal, I returned my attention to the road ahead, determined to put the mummy lady out of my mind. I flipped on my turn signal and slowed at the stop sign. A long blue sedan glided past me, heading in the opposite direction.

The elegant Lincoln Town Car grabbed my attention. I bet it was a smooth ride. The owner of a luxury car, like that, probably never even felt a bump in the road. I just knew it had power steering and power locks. And the radio worked, in the front and the back speakers. Surround sound? How much would an automobile like that cost? How long would I have to eat

Ramen noodles in order to save enough?

What was I thinking? A big car had never been on my wish list. But lately I'd been ogling every pretty car on the road. I knew I should be happy with my free station wagon. It carried me to where I wanted to go. And no payments.

Still admiring the Lincoln, something else grabbed my attention about the lovely blue vehicle—the driver. Perry Sizemore filled the area behind the steering wheel. I held my foot on the brake and stared into the rear-view mirror. Perry passed Utkin's house, traveling almost as slow as I had.

"Why are you cruising this neighborhood, Perry?" I said this to no one. I was in the car alone, without even the cat to talk to.

When the Lincoln drove out of sight, I completed the turn and pulled to the curb. Notebook in hand, I scribbled thoughts as fast as they came. What was Perry's interest in that house? His company wouldn't get the listing. Anita and I knew he was well acquainted with the dead woman. Was he, like me, simply curious about what had happened?

On a more serious note, had he known the woman was dead for the past six months? Had he been waiting for someone to find her? Did he kill her?

Stop it. Don't be crazy.

It was Perry Sizemore, someone I'd known since high-school. He was a well-known business man. Sure, he was a little weird and overly attentive, but not a killer. He'd admitted he knew the woman. He hadn't been strictly forthcoming about how well he knew her. That was understandable, being a married man.

Valentina possessed an incriminating photograph.

Easily a motive for murder. Did she threaten him, or try to blackmail him? How far would a man go to save his reputation and his marriage?

I was deep in thought when the knock vibrated the window. I stifled a scream and tossed the notebook in the air. Perry's face filled the window. He put up his hand in wave and pantomimed lowering the glass.

Now what? Roll down the window, or put my foot on the gas and speed away? Had he seen the lethal questions I'd written? It was then I glanced at the door locks. All the buttons were up. He could have easily opened my door.

For goodness sake Lauren. Pull yourself together. It was broad daylight and on a public street.

Taking a deep breath, I lowered the glass. "Hello Perry. Didn't see you there."

"I saw you drive past me and knew we had to talk. Why don't you come over to my car where we'll be comfortable?"

"Um. Sure. I want to talk to you too. But we might as well sit in the Chrysler since you're already here."

No way would I get into his car. That's how people disappeared.

Perry scanned the interior of my car, and glanced back at his Lincoln. Finally, he walked around the station wagon and climbed in the passenger side. After wedging himself in, he gave a little bounce, rocking the car. "Not bad for an older vehicle."

He twisted his shoulders toward me. "Listen, I know you and Anita saw right through my story about not knowing Valentina. I'll tell you the truth. Our first meeting began exactly as I said. But she seemed so lonely, I sat down, and we talked for quite a while. I felt she hadn't had anyone to confide in for a long time. No family in town. Maybe not even in the country as far as I could tell. No friends."

"You became even better acquainted, didn't you? I think you dated her."

Why did I say that? Did I want to antagonize him? I wanted to stuff my purse in my mouth.

Perry sat up straight. "Who told you?" After a beat, he said, "Oh, you guessed. You're good at that."

When I got my breathing under control, I nodded. "Yes. I guessed."

"And now I've confirmed it. You're one smart woman."

Perry took a breath and forged ahead as though determined to get it all out. "Valentina and I met once or twice in the city. I took her to a nice restaurant. It made her happy to know someone cared. I admit having a beautiful woman on my arm fed my ego. It did a lot for my image."

The big man slumped into the seat. "That was all there was to it, I swear. After the second date, my conscience got to me. I hated the thought of cheating on Marlene. I couldn't sleep for worrying. So, I broke it off with Valentina. Not sure if she believed me, but I assured her I cared. And I did. But it was a bad situation and I told her she needed someone who was free to treat her as she deserved."

"How did she take it?"

"I could tell it broke her heart, but she said she understood."

"How long did the relationship last?"

Perry jerked his head toward me. "It wasn't a relationship. We met a few times, and within a month it was over."

Perry's mood seemed to plummet. I saw anger in his eyes as he stared at me. His cheeks flushed. "As I said, she was a lonely woman. I felt sorry for her."

I slid my left hand to the door handle, hoping it wouldn't fight me if I had to make a quick exit. "I believe you. You were simply being nice to a lonely woman."

He glanced away. "That's right. I shouldn't have taken Valentina to dinner. I know that now." After a moment his eyes darted back to me. "Marlene would be hurt if she ever heard of it. I hope she never does."

I shook my head. "There's nothing to worry about. I promise she won't hear about it from me. We all make mistakes. I've made enough of my own."

He stared at me for a beat, maybe assessing whether he could believe me.

I produced the closest thing to a reassuring smile I could muster. "I was curious. But you've cleared it up. I appreciate you sharing this with me."

Perry straightened in the seat. "Thank you. I'm glad I got it off my chest, and I knew you'd understand." He released his door. "I trust you to keep your promise."

"You can count on me."

Perry hauled himself out of the Chrysler and lumbered to his Lincoln.

My hand still clenched the door handle, and I slowly relaxed my grip. Perry was already in his car, but I stretched over the seat to punch all of the door locks. With a trembling hand I shifted the wagon into drive.

Was Perry simply being kind to Valentina Utkin? I

couldn't help thinking there was more to the relationship than dinner. Did he know about the photo album—her trophy case?

Stop thinking about it. Not your business.

If—when—the truth about Perry's flirtations came out, I didn't want the leak to be traced back to me. To be technical, if Marlene got the news from the Evelynton police department, I would have kept my promise. Wouldn't I?

Those thoughts swirled around in my head for at least ten minutes, before I remembered I was supposed to be driving home. I glanced at the street sign. Maple Drive—three blocks past my turn. I punched the brake, made a left turn and circled the block, determined to pay attention to the road until I was safely at Stoneybridge.

Once inside the house, my thoughts exploded into words, and I scared the cat. "Mason, guess who I saw drive past the mummy woman's house? Perry Sizemore. Then he caught me recording ideas in the notebook. What if he saw what I was writing? Would he misunderstand my interest?"

The feline flattened himself on the floor. When I paused for breath, he stood, executed a sharp u-turn, and galloped from the room. Was my cat psychic? Was it Perry's name that scared him? What did Mason know that I didn't?

I'd lost my mind.

I sat down to take another breath, and to think it through. I hadn't lost my mind. It was more likely low-blood-sugar. All I needed was lunch.

A chicken sandwich brought my blood chemistry into line. Brain-waves back to normal, I spent the remainder of the afternoon editing magazine articles. The street lights were on when I looked up and my stomach was growling again, so I shut down the computer.

After dinner Mason curled up with me on the sofa for an evening of Hitchcock movies.

Given my state of mind, it might not have been a wise choice.

After three classic movies, my eyelids began to droop, so I made my way to the bedroom. Thunder grumbled outside as I turned off the light. After a couple hours of sleep, Valentina Utkin and Perry Sizemore popped into my dreams, startling me awake. All the questions I'd asked myself earlier returned to torment me.

Storms continued to rumble and rain pounded the ground outside. I went to the window in hopes of watching the shower, but it was too dark to catch more than occasional wet reflections. Sporadic flashes of lightning afforded glimpses of the misshapen tree at the center of the lawn.

In one of those flashes, I saw him. The sighting lasted only a couple seconds, but someone was standing in the rain. A man. Or could it have been a woman? Someone lurked on my property. I waited for the next flash of lightning but when it came, the space under the tree was empty. I frantically searched with strained eyes to discover any shape or out-of-place shadow in the glimmering light. My heart thumped against my chest as I reached for the phone. My hand fell on the empty bedside table.

Crap. I'd left the phone in the kitchen.

Taking a deep breath to calm my nerves, I flipped

on the bedroom light. Remembering prowlers were often deterred by house lights, I hit the hall light on the run to the living room. After switching on two table lamps I proceeded to the kitchen. I left the room dark, but hit the switch for the outside light. Then I crept to the window and peered out. No one in sight. Were they at the back of the property, still shrouded in shadow? I waited for another lightning flash. When it came, there was no one in sight.

Creeping back to the kitchen, I fumbled in the darkened room until my hand found the cell phone on the counter. After punching in one number, I stopped. What use would it be to call the police now? The trespasser was gone. Either they were just passing through, or they'd been scared off when they discovered I was awake.

Or I'd imagined it, initiated by the bad dream, and there hadn't been anyone.

With my luck I'd have to talk to Jimmy Farlow. Why was he always on duty when I needed the police? I was in no mood to spend the next hour listening to his dismissive remarks.

Before returning to bed, I stopped at the linen closet and dug under the stack of towels. The Smith & Wesson 442, a gift from my late husband, was stashed at the back. I'd kept it because Marc wanted me to have protection. I'd stashed it under the bath towels because I hated guns. But I pulled it out, checked to confirm that it was loaded and carried it to my bedroom.

Mason occupied the center of the bed, stretched out on his back. He slept soundly.

I could have adopted an orphaned pit bull instead of an entitled cat.

Shoving the feline to the side, I placed the handgun and cell phone side-by-side on the bedside table. After considering leaving the light on, I switched it off. Unlike the cat, I would never be able to sleep with it on. Light from the hallway seeped under the bedroom door as I drifted off to sleep.

~~

The sun was up and a well-rested cat pawed at my face to wake me. Birds played in the left-over rain drops clinging to the leaves outside the window. In the light of the rising sun, the previous night's fright seemed silly. Had I dreamed it? The gun was on the table, so I knew I'd been up. Did I imagine the midnight visitor? That was a possibility. My friends were always teasing me about my imagination.

Mason met me in the kitchen after I emerged from the shower. I filled his bowl and while the coffee-maker worked on its job, I took a stroll outside to breathe the freshly cleansed air. I'd never been an early-riser, but when I woke by accident, the cool morning breeze was a treat. The green vegetation was brighter and the flowers stood taller. The ground squished under-foot.

My stroll came to a halt at the little bush under the bedroom window. After stooping for a closer look, I dashed for the house. My phone lay on the counter next to the coffee pot.

Chapter Seventeen

I dropped the phone, retrieved it, and misdialed twice before I got the numbers in the right order. When I'd succeeded, Wallace's house phone rang five or six times with no answer. I clicked off, inhaled slowly to calm my palpitating heart, and tried his cell. No response. A glance through the living room window confirmed Wallace's truck wasn't in his driveway. He wasn't home.

I knew the next number on my list of emergency contacts would bring an answer. When it didn't, I could only stare at the phone. The connection had broken after two rings. That had to be a mistake. Jack Spencer always responded to my call. I took my time punching in his number once again, making sure to get it right.

The man, who never failed to make me feel safe, answered. "Good morning. Can I call you back in an hour?"

The instant the deep clear voice came through the phone I felt warm and sort of tingly. If there was anything wrong in the world, Jack would fix it.

Words tumbled from my mouth without prelude.

"Jack, someone was in my yard last night. They were lurking by the maple tree, and then they disappeared. You know how it rained? Maybe you didn't get any rain down there, but we did. It came down most of the night. Anyway, someone was out in my back yard, sneaking around the house."

"Um, slow down a little. Who was in your yard? Tell me what you saw."

"Didn't see much. I only got a glimpse of the man—or the person. Could have been a woman, I guess. You see, I woke up in the middle of the night and couldn't go back to sleep. So I was looking out the bedroom window, you know, trying to relax and get sleepy. The storm was coming in and lightning flashed. That's when I saw a figure standing by the tree out back. But when the yard lit up the next time, they were gone! I didn't know what to do. Couldn't go back to sleep with some stranger on the property."

I paused to catch my breath and charged ahead. "So I went through the house and turned on lights. Then I turned on the outside light. I figured it was the right thing to do and hoped it would scare them away. That plan seemed to work, but now I think maybe it didn't. This morning I went out back and found footprints in the mud. Someone was snooping all around the back of the house and right up next to the windows."

"Could've been kids, or a peeping Tom. You close your curtains don't you?"

"Sure. I always shut the draperies and lock the windows. It was raining hard, quite a shower, so I can't imagine a peeping Tom staying out in it to peek in my windows. I'm not that exciting."

"You might be surprised. I'll have to call you b—"

"Anyway, I was so scared I left the lights on all night."

Jack sighed. I heard it through the receiver. "Did you call the police?"

"No. You know my relationship with our police department. Don't you remember my encounters with Officer Farlow? I'll only call him if I'm in mortal danger."

"I guess I can't blame you. So, what did Wallace say?"

"He isn't home. I tried his cell and he didn't answer. I talked myself out of worrying last night, but this morning, the foot prints have me creeped out. I didn't know what to do, but I had faith you would."

"I'm afraid you'll have to speak to the Evelynton Police Department, or wait until Wallace gets home to see what he says. You know I would help, but I'm three hours away and working on a case."

"Working? Right now?"

He lowered his voice. "Yes. I'm interviewing a client. He's sort of an important client."

I lowered my voice to a whisper. "Oh. They're in your office now?"

"No. I'm in his office. The mayor's office."

Crap.

"The mayor. I'm so sorry. Better let you go. I'll wait for Wallace. Now that I think about it, it's probably nothing anyway. Sorry for bothering you. Say hello to the mayor. No, don't do that. Um, talk to you later. Bye." I clicked off without waiting for Jack's reply.

I carried my coffee to the table, pulled out a chair and plopped into it. Mason crouched at my feet, and I leaned over to gaze into his eyes. "Why didn't you warn me? I should have thought it over before I made that call. Maybe I should have had a cup of coffee first? Jack was right. It was probably a harmless peeping Tom who doesn't know enough to stay out of the rain."

My cat leapt into my lap and rubbed his head on my chin. "Too late to apologize. You already let me embarrass myself. And all because I got freaked out over some misguided soul."

I shoved the cat from my lap, and sipped hot coffee. Who would have stood in the rain outside my house that night? Could it have been someone I knew?

Was it Perry Sizemore? He'd made it obvious he'd had designs on me—and a few other women in town—but a peeping tom? No way would he brave the weather for a thrill. Unless of course, there was more to the story of him and Valentina.

Wait. The shadow wasn't large enough or round enough to be Perry.

Who else? I took a long slurp of coffee, weighing the possibilities.

What about Ted the handyman? He'd been inside my house, and all over the property. But he was a nice man and never anything less than polite. Although he was clean cut when I'd first met him. Neglecting haircuts and shaving shouldn't make him a suspect.

Who else? Wallace Binion? He'd been acting strange lately, but he was the last person who'd be sneaking around my property. No, not Wallace. He'd helped me on countless occasions.

That left someone I didn't know. A stranger. Probably some kid, or a drifter. Not dangerous. There was nothing to be worried about.

By lunchtime I'd managed to stay focused on my writing long enough to finish an assignment. It was a beautiful portrayal of life in a small town. I'd put the Norman Rockwell lifestyle into words. Right down to the lovely moonlit walks on quiet streets. I was careful to include the security of living in a community of friends and family. Where there were no strangers within fifteen square miles. Tranquil, calm, no worries.

So I'd drifted into fiction. It's what sold magazines.

Satisfied I'd created a masterpiece that would pay the bills, I placed a call to Anita. Best to seek another opinion of my spooky backyard visitor.

"You'll never guess what went on here last night."

After repeating the story, I had to admit it seemed to be a tale concocted of my absurd imagination. Anita wasn't laughing at me, so I confessed to calling Jack Spencer and not giving him a chance to tell me he was busy.

"Now the man thinks I'm not only out of my mind, but a pest as well."

"I wouldn't worry about it. So you're excitable sometimes, he knows how you are."

"Excitable?" I thought she could have been more encouraging. Spontaneous, would have been a good description.

"Not in a bad way. Besides, he'll overlook it because he's smitten with you."

"Smitten? Do you think so?"

"Of course he is. Why else would he drive all the way up here to spend time with you? Besides, I've seen the look on the man's face when you're together."

"It's nice to think about. But he lives and works

three hours away. That makes it impossible to build any kind of relationship."

I thought about that word for a moment. "Wait. I'm not sure I even want him closer. I'm not ready for the relationship thing. It's important that I'm able to take care of myself before I fit someone else into the equation. The way I lost control this morning proves I'm still much too needy. I'd wear the guy out."

"Hmm. Guess you're right."

Still waiting for the encouraging words.

"Tonight will be good for you. Clair called, didn't she?"

"Yes, she told me about the movie party. But you know I'm not good at large gatherings, and I don't watch romance movies."

"Give it a chance. It's just some of the girls stopping over for snacks and Hallmark movies. You know almost everyone. Clair's hosting it at my house because her apartment is too small."

"It's hard to believe Clair would take time away from work for anything, let alone to watch romance movies."

"Yes, I know. Isn't it great? She's making some changes, enjoying life more. Something you should do, too. But we're firm on romantic flicks, no mysteries or suspense. I think it's perfect timing. You could use a break from cops and robbers. Let's watch something sweet and happy."

"There's never anything to think about in those movies. You always know how it's going to work out and who gets the girl—after the one heart-breaking misunderstanding."

"Exactly. Isn't it comforting? That's why I love

them."

"I thought you'd become a mystery buff."

"Only in short bouts. I love happy endings, don't you? Come over. We'll have fun."

~~

That evening, I said good-bye to Mason on my way out. "Keep the sofa warm for me. I'll be gone an hour at most. Planning an early exit, just before the sappy movies start."

Anita's rambling farmhouse sat three miles out of town. Towering sunflowers swayed at the side of the house. A long, fruit-tree-lined lane led to the house. The scene was a picture of domestic bliss, right out of one of those darn romance movies. Anita and her husband, Jake, weren't farmers, even though they had a nice vegetable garden. The out-buildings, that completed the farming picture, housed rakes, barbecue grill, and snow mobiles.

When I stepped out of the car, two over-weight Golden Retrievers galloped to greet me. After slobbering on my hand, they followed me to the house, tails wagging and tongues hanging. The party sounded as if it was in full swing inside, so I opened the door to let myself in. The crowded living room—more women than I'd expected—almost moved me to beat a fast retreat. But Clair caught sight of me before I could slip out. "Lauren, you're here."

Anita's third monster dog, a chocolate lab named Gordon, lay in the middle of the room. His head remained flat on the floor and his tail thumped as I stepped over him. I made my way to the sofa where Clair sat beside a woman wearing jeans and a fluffy blue blouse. I didn't know her. In fact, most of the guests were strangers to me.

I passed Patricia Martin, dress shop owner. Her stylish sweater and slacks must have been among the newest arrivals at her shop. The woman beside her seemed familiar, and I should have remembered her name, but hadn't a clue. Patricia broke off her conversation to introduce me to Francis somebody, who worked at the post office.

I moved on and did a double-take at a woman slumped into an overstuffed chair in the corner. "Hi, Ava. Hardly recognized you outside of the Java." She smiled and mouthed the word "Hi" before resting her head on the back of the chair. I was pretty sure she'd be asleep soon.

Irma, the police station file clerk, perched on a footstool next to Ava. She took a sip from her wine glass and shrugged. "Ava gets up early to open the coffee shop."

Anita poked her head out from the kitchen and called above the chatter. "So glad you made it. I think you know everyone, except maybe Cindy." She pointed to the woman beside Clair. "She's an old friend. First person I met when I started attending First Evangelical. We've been great friends ever since."

I did my best to imitate someone who was happy to be part of the group. Even participated in small-talk while squeezed into the end of the sofa, next to Clair.

Gordon maintained sentinel in the center of the room. His brown eyes followed Anita while she stepped over and around him, to hand Clair an iced-tea.

"What can I get you? We have tea, coffee, pop, two kinds of wine—sweet or dry."

I requested tea. My mind already constructing a

believable excuse for early departure.

Clair leaned toward Cindy. "Lauren is a writer. She's the top contributor to several big magazines. We're so proud of her."

"That's exciting. Tell me about your writing. I can't imagine how you know what to write about. Where do you get your ideas?"

I explained that ideas were always floating around in my head, mostly about mysterious murders. Cindy smiled and focused on Clair, to ask about her health.

Someone flipped the television on and sweet romantic music filled the room. I turned away so I wouldn't get drawn into the plot. I ended up facing Irma.

"Have they learned anything new about the death of your neighbor?"

"Melvin says it was suicide, so he's done working on it."

"How did he determine that? Did they get the forensics back?"

"Nope. He says there wasn't any evidence to the contrary, and he's been in the business long enough to trust his gut." Irma leaned toward me. "Personally, I think he needs an antacid."

"How much experience has Melvin had? I know he's experienced in basic law enforcement but how many unexplained deaths have there been in Evelynton? Nothing ever happens in this quiet little village."

Irma raised her eyebrows.

I back-tracked. "Well, there was that murder right after I moved back to town. And Patsy tried to shoot me. And then the body in the ravine, about a year later.

I did almost get shot before that one was solved. But before that, Evelynton hadn't had any homicides. Had they?"

"Wasn't that enough?" Irma drained her glass and held it up to Anita for a refill.

Didn't have an answer to that, so I shrugged. "You haven't heard anything else about the body in the garage?"

"Nope. Case closed. Can't wait until someone else moves into that house. They can take care of the lawn."

Patricia had been listening to our exchange. She chimed in with, "I think I met the mummy woman last year. A woman was in my shop and her name was something funny. Might have been Utkin. She bought several of my higher priced dresses. Had me wondering where she was going to wear them. I only keep them in stock to make my inventory look better." She drained her wine glass. "I had to dust them off before she tried them on."

"That's interesting. Did she say why she wanted the dresses? What did she talk about?"

"I don't think she mentioned where she planned to wear elegant frocks like those. Really don't think we discussed anything in particular. I was happy to get them sold."

Ava woke up and lurched forward in her chair. Blinking at me, she said, "Hi Lauren. When did you get here?" I smiled back at her bleary grin and she turned to Patricia. "I almost forgot to ask. Did you get my support hose in?"

I let the two of them discuss the advantages of vein support, and turned my attention to Clair. "Are you crying? What's wrong?"

She pointed at the television and sniffed. "Chrissy and Phil broke up. She said their lifestyles were too different. She's a farm girl and he's a big city attorney, but I can tell they really need each other."

"Don't worry. I'm sure they'll get back together."

"Do you think so?"

Two hours later I pushed myself off the sofa and said my good-byes, hugging Anita at the door. I had to admit she'd been right. I walked out refreshed after a pleasant evening. It had been stress-free—except for Clair's tears over two fictional characters.

Like parking attendants, two dogs met me at the door and escorted me to the station wagon. I rewarded each with a pat on the head and climbed into the Chrysler.

An unexplainable peace had settled over the land. Clouds obscured the night sky. Not a sign of the moon or a star. My headlights barely pierced the darkness on the country roads. The dark roads and lack of visible landmarks should have worried me, but I found it soothing. I reached Evelynton city limits and followed the street lights toward home.

Like most small towns, stores had closed at nine, and there were very few cars on the road. I motored past the quiet and darkened Rare Curl. Ava's Java seemed a bit lonely. Closed sign on the door and no line waiting for a caffeine fix. Shops were shuttered and streets were deserted as I cruised down the main corridor of my hometown.

I made a left turn onto Stoneybridge. Some soul was out for a lonely walk. A blue light flickered through curtains in the front room of the Baron's house. I imagined Clive and Murine next to each other on the sofa, watching the late news. On the other side of my Cape Cod, Wallace's truck sat in his driveway, but his windows were dark. He'd turned in early.

My headlights illuminated the small concrete porch of my house. The outside lights had been left off since I'd planned to be home before sunset. I cut the engine and trotted up the steps to make my way inside. A small antique lamp, one of the few of Aunt Ruth's I'd kept, lit up the room at the flip of a switch. I stood frozen by the door and stared.

Chapter Eighteen

An empty bookshelf taunted me from the opposite wall. My papers and reference volumes littered the floor. I leaned in and scanned the living and dining rooms. Chaos.

Mason crept out from under the sofa, his round, golden eyes staring up at me.

"Thank goodness, you're okay." I stooped to scoop the trembling kitty into my arms, and held him close. Switching on the overhead light in the dining room, I took in the extent of the damage. Drawers gaped open in the corner china cabinet. One of Aunt Ruth's precious plates lay broken on the rug.

The kitchen cupboard doors stood ajar, displaying the contents. Wandering back to the living room, I gazed into the bedroom and wondered if I should investigate upstairs. But I came to my senses and stopped myself before going further.

I whispered, "Are they still here?" And tucking the cat under my arm, I grabbed my bag from the end table and fled to the car. Safely locked inside I pulled out my cell phone.

The emergency operator asked me to speak up as I reported my home had been violated, and the perpetrator might still be inside. She stayed on the line with me for the five minutes it took a squad car to pull up behind my Chrysler. A second parked on the street. A policeman stood by my window. At the sight of a friendly face, I lowered the glass half-way. I recognized this man as Amos Smith, the kindly officer who'd accompanied Farlow when we reported the mummified woman. He instructed me to roll the window up, and to stay in the car while he checked out the premises. I put up no argument. The second officer, who I thought must be about sixteen, followed Amos into the house. I waited. Lights became visible in the upstairs windows. Later I saw flashlights in the backyard. I was getting antsy by the time Amos returned to my window and motioned for me to put it down.

"It's okay. You can come out now. There's no one around. They jimmied the back door. Not the bolt-lock, the regular door lock. Looks like they went through everything. Sorry, they left quite a mess."

Crap. I forgot to set the dead-bolt again. I'd begun to believe my own writing about the safety of small towns.

Officer Smith filled out a report and I signed it. "When you're able to go through your stuff and put it away, you can let us know what's missing."

He started to return to his squad car but stopped. "Do you want me to go into the house with you? Maybe you'll feel more secure." I'm pretty sure I looked like a lost puppy when my head bobbed an affirmative.

Amos waved the younger officer on. "Go on ahead. I'll be along shortly."

I deposited Mason on the sofa when we stepped back inside the house, but he jumped down and stayed by my ankle as the officer and I toured every room and every closet. I almost apologized to the policeman for the mess, until I remembered this wasn't my doing.

I secured the back door and let Officer Smith double-check it. As soon as he stepped onto the front porch, I threw the bolt lock. I wondered if he'd listened for the tell-tale click.

Mason had stayed by my side, with his tail curled around my ankle. "I don't have the energy to fix this. Let's do my bedroom and bath tonight. We'll work on the rest in the morning." I knew he wasn't going to do any work—he's a cat. I'd lived alone long enough to find comfort in pretending I had a roommate.

All energy I'd gained at Clair's party gone, I trudged to the bedroom. Mason learned a new game as I folded clothes and tucked them into drawers. He crawled into the drawer with every new deposit, and stayed long enough to leave cat hair, before I pulled him out. Then, he waited patiently for the next item, and hopped in again.

The lights stayed on again that night. The month's electric bill would be a challenge.

We crawled into bed. "Mason, why didn't you remind me to tell Officer Smith about the prowler in the back yard? I'll have to tell him tomorrow." I grabbed the cat and tucked him under the covers with me. He struggled loose and curled up on my pillow.

~~

Sunshine cut through the bedroom window. Another beautiful day. This pleasant moment lasted only until I remembered the mess that awaited me. I thought I would snuggle in and sleep a while longer, but my aggravating cat had other plans. He pawed at the sheet to uncover my ear, so he could torment me with his sandpaper tongue.

I pushed him off the bed. "Okay, I'm up."

While the coffee brewed, I replaced dishes and straightened the cabinets. Mason was particularly worried about the bag of cat food the intruder left in the middle of the kitchen floor. I filled his bowl and returned the bag to the pantry. While there, I organized the canned goods. Next I replaced pots and pans under the counter.

"Look, Mason, even vandalism has a silver-lining. This kitchen hasn't been cleaned and organized since I moved in."

"At least they didn't touch the silverware drawer. Why do you think that is?" Having eaten his fill, the cat was no longer interested. He'd found a sunny patch in the dining room and stretched out for a snooze.

This reminded me I had to get to work. The rest of the mess would have to wait until afternoon. I rushed out the door and drank my coffee on the fly.

On my way to The Rare Curl, I breezed into the police station to tell them I hadn't found anything missing, so far. And I didn't know why I'd forgotten to tell Officer Smith about the prowler, but it might be important.

As I stepped through the station door, I scanned the room searching for Amos Smith. Par for the course, Jimmy Farlow stood in the middle of the office with his eyes laser-focused on me.

"Ms. Halloren. What sort of catastrophe have you had already this morning? Found another body? Maybe you're chasing bank robbers?"

Inhaling slowly, I smiled at my least favorite person in Evelynton. "Good morning, Officer Farlow. Is Amos Smith around?"

"No. What do you want?"

"You may not have heard. Someone broke into my house last night. Officer Smith asked me to stop by to let him know what was stolen. I haven't found anything missing so far, but I wanted to tell him I saw someone prowling around my back yard the night before the break-in. They were even next to my windows. I saw footprints."

"This event occurred day before yesterday? Did you see who it was?"

"No. It was dark and raining."

"Why didn't you report it then? How do you expect us to do anything about it now? You people expect us to perform miracles while you sit back, never lifting a finger." He pivoted and walked toward his desk. "Forget about it. It was most likely kids anyway."

Watching him walk away, I stuttered, "I didn't report it then because…. I don't know why I didn't report it. Guess it didn't seem important, but after the break-in…"

Still with his back to me, he raised his voice. "We've had some trouble with vandals in town. You're the latest victim. My advice is to clean it up, lock your doors, and forget about it. I'll tell Officer Smith you were in. As for alleging someone trespassing in your yard. Happens all the time. Somebody wandered in and wandered out. It isn't significant. Goodbye."

"Um. Okay." I grabbed the door handle. I hadn't stepped inside the door more than a few inches, so it was an easy escape.

I dove into the comfort of my Chrysler, and took Main Street to The Rare Curl. As I drove I pondered who would take the trouble to break in and not steal anything. Of course, there was the possibility they simply didn't like any of my stuff.

By the time I'd reached the salon, I agreed with Officer Farlow. It must have been vandals out to cause mischief. Who else would have any desire to break into my humble little house?

Chapter Nineteen

Three wine glasses clinked together as I gingerly balanced them while pushing through the screen door to the back porch. Anita had made herself comfortable, propping her feet against the side railing. Clair held Mason on her lap. I wondered if she noticed the black and white hairs clinging to her navy skirt.

I handed Clair her Chardonnay. "Looks like you'll need a lint brush before you leave."

She accepted the glass and hugged Mason closer. "Not to worry. His hair brushes off easily enough. And a little bit of hair doesn't bother me. I can't wait to live in a house where I can have a pet, maybe two."

I smiled at my inexperienced friend.

Wait 'til she finds fuzzies in the refrigerator.

Anita took a sip from the glass I handed her. "Clair Lane, I never thought I'd see the day when you'd be holding an animal while still wearing your suit."

Anita winked at me. "Do you think she's having a midlife crisis?"

Clair gasped. "Don't even think those words. We aren't that old." Mason, who'd had enough hugging, took the opportunity to bound from her lap and escape through his cat-door.

I watched him scamper across the yard, and then gazed through the screen at the dirt beneath my bedroom window. "I haven't found any more footprints."

Clair brushed cat hair from her skirt. "There wouldn't be any, would there? We've had rain the last three nights."

Anita put her feet on the floor for a better view of the area. "Stop worrying, I'm sure it was only someone wandering around the neighborhood. Some people like to walk in the rain."

"Through my backyard? And they thought they'd stand under my window?"

She shrugged. "Creepy, I know. There are lonely people who have nothing better to do."

"Umm. And someone just happened to break in to my house."

Clair picked a cat hair from her wine glass. "Well, that is strange. But they didn't take anything. And you weren't home."

"I wouldn't be concerned. Just a prank." Anita leaned back in her chair and closed her eyes.

I stared at my relaxed friend. Why did no one take me seriously? I wasn't overreacting, was I?

With a deep breath I collapsed into a chair. "I don't want to talk about it anymore."

"Good. Let's think of something else." Anita leaned her head toward me and whispered. "I talked to Irma at the party. Asked her if the police had gone back to the mummy house. She said they hadn't and weren't planning to. They figured the death was from natural causes, and not worth the time. Too busy."

"I don't think we can let them do that. We know it means something."

Clair leaned into our huddle. "What means something? What are you talking about?"

I glanced up. "We didn't want to tell you."

"Why wouldn't you tell me—your best friend?"

"You'll understand, soon."

Anita filled her in on our ill-advised adventure, and I watched Clair's face morph through several stages of horror.

"You didn't! Why would you do that? You might have been caught. Then I'd have to go in and try to bail you out. I suppose I could get into my savings." Wine sloshed from her glass as she gasped. "They would never let me buy the house after that. Everyone knows we're friends."

I gave her arm a pat. "We got in and out without being caught. The only problem we have, now, is what to do about the evidence. It wouldn't be right to keep quiet."

Anita bobbed her head. "We have to tell the police. If we don't, it's the sin of omission—failing to do something we should."

Clair chugged the rest of the wine. "I can't believe it. They'll put you both in jail. Probably blame me, too."

She leaned back in her chair with her hand on her forehead.

"It isn't that bad. It's…" Anita's voice faded. She gazed at Clair, then at me.

I put my hands up. "I've decided. I'll take care of it today. Irma will get an anonymous note with the information. Then she'll take it to the police chief. We won't be implicated, and you know Irma will love it. She'll feel very important."

Anita's eyes got big. "That'll work." She paused. I could almost hear the brain cells ticking. "Um. Wear rubber gloves when you handle the note and the envelope."

"I doubt our police force will think to look for finger prints. But I'll wear gloves."

Clair placed her wine glass on the floor. "If you're set on this plan, make sure no one knows who you are."

"Don't worry. It'll be completely anonymous." I was pretty sure Clair was more concerned with the house than with our jail time.

"I could bypass Irma and just send the note to the police station. What do you think?"

It took a minute, but Anita popped up with the answer. "Nope. The more hands it goes through, the more likely any trace evidence will be contaminated. They'll be less likely to follow it back to you."

Clair rolled her eyes. "I wish you'd give up the mystery novels."

Anita spun toward me, eyes wide. "What if Irma thinks it's a joke and throws the note away? Or what if the chief doesn't believe it?"

I massaged my temples. "I don't know. My brain is tired. Let's just wait and see if we get a reaction."

Anita's eyes flashed. "If nothing happens after a few days I'll go to the police myself."

I shook my head hard enough to make myself dizzy. "No you won't. Jake would be furious with you. And with me. I'll go. If anyone gets arrested, it should be me. It's my responsibility."

Chapter Twenty

It was a simple note. Should have been easy enough.

I flung one more wadded page toward the trash. Doing his best Michael Jordon impersonation, Mason leapt, intercepted the paper ball, and batted it to the side. As soon as it hit the floor, he pounced on it. "Hey, I meant that for the waste basket. Put it back." He trotted from the room with it in his mouth.

Impudent cat.

I gave composing another try. Just the facts—no clues as to the author. Discarding one draft after another, I created half a dozen paper cat toys.

At last, I produced believable words and printed them in large block letters. Remembering Anita's advice, I ran to the kitchen sink to retrieve yellow rubber dish-washing gloves, then grabbed another sheet to write the note without fingerprints.

TAKE THIS TO THE POLICE
THERE IS EVIDENCE PERTAINING TO THE DEATH OF THE UTKIN WOMAN IN HER HOUSE.

IT MIGHT PROVE THERE WAS A MURDER. SEARCH THE HOUSE AND ESPECIALLY THE DRAWERS. LOOK FOR A PHOTO ALBUM
   SINCERELY
   CONCERNED CITIZEN

   I scrapped that letter and wrote another with MUMMY in place of UTKIN. In a flash of paranoia I became certain someone would recognize my printing, so I wadded up that draft, and tossed it to the waste basket. Then, I set about gathering old magazines, and pulled a pair of scissors from the kitchen junk drawer.
   Finding and cutting letters—and even full words—from the magazines proved to be easy. That part of the job was finished in less than ten minutes, but the difficulty level shot up as I attempted to glue the bits of paper onto a fresh sheet of typing paper. By the time I'd finished everything, note, gloves, table, my face, and hair, was smeared with glue. The note, meant as a credible piece of evidence, resembled a child's preschool project. But it was readable, mostly, and I was pretty sure no one would link it to me.
   I laid the note aside to dry and pulled an envelope from my desk, along with a few spares. I ruined three in my gluing attempts before scrapping the idea and hand printing the address. The post office needed to be able to read it.
   My work wasn't finished yet. The postage stamp was another challenge. Still wearing my yellow kitchen gloves, grumbling a lot, and cussing a little, I succeeded in affixing it near the corner of the envelope.
   My first impulse, after sealing the envelope with the note inside, was to run it to a mailbox. But wisdom

dictated I wait until fewer people roamed the streets. I paced until sundown, jumped in the wagon and found a mailbox eight blocks from my house. I pulled the Chrysler close to the curb, left the motor running, and dashed to the box. Returning to the car, a scan of the street revealed no witnesses. Hopefully no one stared out their window, wondering why the strange woman might be wearing one yellow kitchen glove.

Back at home, I prayed the letter, soiled and crumpled as it was from the fight with the stamp, wouldn't land in the hands of a judgmental postal employee, and that it would actually be delivered. Later, I prayed Irma would take the information seriously. Then I prayed the police would consider it a credible tip, even though possibly submitted by a four-year-old. Would they perform a thorough search of the house? Should I have told them exactly where to look? I scratched my head, thinking there were a lot of variables in my plan.

Slumping onto the sofa, I lay my head on the cushion determined to put the letter out of my mind for three days. Two days to reach Irma, and another for her to deliver it to the station.

How would we know if the search had taken place? I could ask Irma, but would she question why I wanted to know? Better to send Anita. She could ask questions without raising suspicion. No one ever suspected Anita.

~~

Rising early the next morning, I felt lighter than I had since making the ill-advised trip to that woman's house. My responsibility was in the mail.

I needed to expend excess energy and to stop trying to master every puzzle, so I put on my sneakers. I planned to leave the Chrysler at home and set out for work on foot. It was time to appreciate the changing leaf colors, the flowers, and the birds. I'd enjoy the morning. I'd leave the Evelynton police force to solve the final mystery—a conundrum that was no longer my business.

"I'll see you this afternoon, Mason."

The cat looked up from his bowl and responded with a simple "Mew."

When I flung the front door open I almost jumped out of my sneakers. I stood face to friendly face with Amos Smith, his fist poised to pound the door.

His smile was broad and kind. He never scared me, as did his co-worker, Jimmy Farlow. "Hi, Officer Smith. Some timing, huh? What can I do for you?"

"Good morning, Ms. Halloren. Do you have a few minutes?"

"Sure. You just caught me on my way to work, but I have time. Come in."

Amos stepped in and planted his fists on his hips. "I received a report of a prowler on your property. Maybe a vagrant? It stated you found foot-prints?"

Good grief. How long does it take a complaint to circulate the Evelynton police department?

Before I had a chance to respond that he was much too late to see any evidence, Mason trotted into the room with a wadded paper ball in his mouth, and dropped it at the officer's feet.

I got a little dizzy.

"Hi, kitty." Amos leaned over, picked up the ball and gave it a toss. He chuckled as Mason scampered away and caught the ball, batting it to the corner. "I love cats. You never know what they're going to do."

I took a couple giant steps to grab the wadded anonymous note. "Crazy cat. Always stealing paper from the waste basket. He'd have trash all over the house if I let him."

I stuffed the paper into my pocket and returned to Officer Smith. "About the foot-prints, I should have reported it when you were here before, but forgot. Anyway, they're gone now. Washed away by the three days of rain we had. I'm sorry you had to waste your time driving over."

From the corner of my eye, I noticed Mason strutting in from the kitchen with another waded paper ball.

The cat hates me.

Mason sat at Officer Smith's feet, staring up with adoring kitten eyes. Before I had a chance to intervene, Amos accepted the ball and gave it a toss.

"Sorry, I know I shouldn't have done that. But he's so cute, the way he bats it around. He should be on a soccer team."

My aggravating cat seized the paper and trotted back to his new friend. Before I could confiscate it, Amos gave it a toss across the room.

A silent prayer ran through my mind. "God, I'm sorry I broke into that house. Please don't let the officer see what's written on the paper and arrest me."

Amos had crouched down, once more, to continue his new game with Mason.

I held out my hand and lowered my voice, trying to sound firm. "I'll throw that away. We don't want to encourage bad behavior, do we?"

Once again Amos threw it into the dining room for Mason to chase. "Gosh, I'm sorry. I couldn't help myself. I hate to take it away from him. But I guess you need rules, even with pets." Mason volleyed the ball back to Amos. He picked up the paper and looked at it as if he might throw it. I held my breath. He chuckled and handed it to me—still wadded. "I guess, being a writer, you would have lots of paper around. Can't let the little fella play with all of it. You'd have quite a mess in the house."

I snatched it from him and stuffed it into my pocket. Mason grumbled and bounded to the kitchen.

Meanwhile Officer Smith stood and put his hand on the door knob. "Guess I better get back to work."

"Once again, I'm sorry you had to drive over here for nothing."

"Not at all. I had fun playing with your kitty." He pulled open the door and stepped onto the porch.

I noticed Mason at my feet, yet another paper ball in his teeth. I bid Officer Smith good-bye and yanked the paper from the cat's mouth.

When the door was shut, I leveled my gaze at my pesky pet. "Where did you hide these? Are you trying to get me arrested?"

Mason stalked from the room, tail in the air. I called after him, "When I get home, I'm conducting a thorough search to see if you have more."

I gathered my handbag and stepped onto the porch, my mood considerably less carefree than it had been earlier. Had Amos Smith seen the large printed words inside the note? When they received the letter at the station, would the memory be triggered?

Speed-walking toward the salon, I neglected to appreciate the colorful leaves, the birds, and the sunshine. How many trial pages had I discarded? Were there more in the house? What if Mason had carried one outside?

Chapter Twenty-One

Screeching tires and a blaring car horn set my heart pounding and had me frozen in place. "Watch where you're going, woman! You wanna get yourself killed?"

Crap. I'd marched right out into oncoming traffic. On my stroll to work, I'd not only forgotten to admire nature, as I'd planned, but I'd become so distracted I'd missed the transition between residential and downtown Evelynton.

I waved at the aggravated man at the wheel. "Sorry, Clive. I'll pay more attention." Grumpy seemed to be Clive Barron's natural mood. It occurred to me to be grateful he'd decided to apply the brakes. I trotted to the opposite curb, and he drove away without further comment.

Paying careful attention to speeding cars and other pitfalls, I continued into town, and got to within two blocks of The Rare Curl when I heard the commotion. At first, heated voices mingled with morning traffic sounds. The words were unclear, but they flew from the alley beside the drugstore. As I drew nearer, shouts rang out louder and a few expressions were recognizable. An angry debate.

I told myself to keep walking. Whatever the reason for the argument—not my concern. But never being good at minding my own business, I skidded to a stop and inched toward the entrance to stare into the dimly lit lane. As my eyes grew accustomed to the shadows, two people materialized at the back of the alley, engaged in animated conversation. At my first glance I thought, Ellen Felicity. My eyes were deceiving me. The dead end lane, with its grime and garbage cans, wasn't a place Miss Perfect would hang out. But who else stood that tall and pencil thin, and wore a bob haircut?

I couldn't tear myself away from the sparring. Had the man forced the woman between the buildings? Was she in danger? He could have out-weighed her by a hundred pounds.

In one pivot and wild swing of her arms, a beam of sunlight reflected on her hair. Blond. So pale it practically glowed. Definitely Ellen Felicity, and as a coworker, I was duty bound to assist her.

I crept further into the alley, planning an attack. I scanned the area for a weapon, but finding none, would rely on a surprise move. The minute the man touched her, I'd storm in and tackle him. He was really big, but between the two of us, Ellen and I would be able to fight him off, I hoped.

In an unexpected move, Ellen put her shoulders back and planted her hands on her hips. The simple gesture silenced the man. His shoulders slumped and he backed away.

She spun on her heal and began to stalk from the

alley, aimed right at me. *Yikes.* Fortunately for me, her eyes were on the ground, so I scampered a retreat and hit the sidewalk running. What explanation would I have for spying on Ellen Felicity? Nothing she would believe.

Once inside The Rare Curl I threw my bag into a cabinet and slid into the desk chair. Ellen would arrive at any minute, so I did some deep breathing and thought sweet thoughts. I hoped to appear settled, as if I'd been there for hours.

About two minutes later, Ellen stormed in and marched to her styling station. She ignored my practiced greeting. Nothing new there. Instead, she proceeded to pull open drawers and slam brushes onto the counter.

Dying to know the story of the guy in the alley, I could barely contain myself. As a distraction, I bit my tongue and counted customers on the appointment book. I whispered into the book, "Her business, not mine. What happened in the alley stays in the alley."

No one ever said I had great self-control. Words sometimes popped out of my mouth of their own accord. "Is everything alright, Ellen?"

She jerked her head toward me as if surprised to see me in the room. Her eyes widened and focused. "Of course. Everything is fine. Why wouldn't it be?"

"Oh no reason. I thought you seemed a little distracted. Might have had a problem on the way in to work. Car trouble? Or were you hassled by someone? A mugger?"

"No." She tipped her head to the side and blew out a sigh. "What are you talking about?" The woman thought I'd lost my mind. She picked up a hairbrush and studied it for stray hairs.

I chuckled. "How silly of me. I saw you walk in, and car trouble popped into my head. I don't even know what you drive or if you even have a car. You might walk to work. Do you?"

Ellen let out another sigh as she wrenched her head toward me. "No I don't walk to work. I drive." She took two cans of hairspray from the shelf and arranged them on her styling station.

"Oh. Has anyone ever hassled you between your parking place and the salon? You never know who might be out there."

Lord, help me stop babbling.

Ellen's silver blond locks fanned out as she spun toward me. She stared as if I'd sprouted antlers. Apparently she decided the feeble-minded receptionist didn't warrant a response. Her lips formed a tight line while she grabbed a towel to dust her work station.

I thought I might ask again. Having already come across as a complete idiot, what did I have to lose? But thankfully, Rarity chose that moment to bounce out of the supply room. "Good morning ladies. This is the day the Lord has made! The sun is shining and our appointment books are full. We are all healthy and happy. God is good."

That ended my poor attempt at investigation. I'd wait, and think of another angle.

Later, after cashing out a customer, I saw my chance. Ellen wielded a broom around the base of her styling chair. Rarity stood in the waiting room, conducting an inventory of items on the retail shelf. I swiveled my chair to face Ellen.

"I'm sorry if I upset you earlier. Really didn't

mean to pry. You seemed to be upset when you came in. I thought you'd possibly had some sort of confrontation."

The look on Ellen's face caused me to rethink my plan. In fact, I thought I might excuse myself and dash to the ladies room.

Saved by the ringing of the telephone. "Oops, better get that." I spun around, grabbed the receiver, hunched my shoulders against attack, and concentrated on the appointment book.

After finishing with the caller, I peeked over my shoulder. Ellen worked on a comb-out and seemed to be over-heated or maybe she'd applied too much blush. Our normally ice cold and self-possessed hairdresser dropped her comb twice and fumbled the hair spray. After sending her customer to me, Ellen stomped to the ladies room. Her signature model-strut, noticeably absent.

When she returned, she seemed to have pulled herself together, but stopped to speak to Rarity. "I have no more appointments scheduled, and will be taking the rest of the day off."

"Of course dear, are you unwell?"

"You are so perceptive, Mrs. Peabody. I'm not feeling at all well. I suppose I've contracted a virus. A rest will be good for me." She scooped all of her combs and brushes into a drawer, slid it shut, with more force than necessary, and marched toward the exit.

I felt the breeze as she passed. "Good-bye. Hope you feel better." Was the man in the alley the cause of the sudden virus, or was I?

Chapter Twenty-Two

Ellen's encounter in the alley was still fresh in my mind on my way to Ava's Java, the next morning. I slipped past the drugstore alley with only a quick peak. Nothing happening among the garbage cans. Not that I expected it be a regular meeting place for Ellen and her friend.

At Ava's my thoughts soon turned to the scent of bacon. The early morning crowd sat munching on gourmet breakfast sandwiches.

I shook my head as I stepped up to our usual table, where Clair and Anita were already into their first cup of coffee. "I don't understand how you two always get here ahead of me."

"I'm here early because those dogs woke up at five a.m. but I think Clair lives here. The Java is her second office. I'm wondering when Ava will start charging her rent."

I hung my handbag over the back of the chair reserved for me. "What are you girls having this morning?"

Anita smiled. "I ordered bacon, scrambled egg, and

white cheddar on Ciabatta. Sounds wonderful doesn't it? I love it when someone else cooks breakfast. It makes me feel like I'm on vacation."

Clair put a hand on her stomach and shook her head. "Fruit and Greek yogurt for me. Been putting on a little weight."

I grabbed my credit card and trotted to the counter to search the menu, but was too distracted to make a decision. "Just give me what Anita's having." Ava handed me my coffee and I hustled to the table.

I broke into my friends' conversation. "Wait 'til I tell you what I saw on the way to work yesterday. You remember the new hairdresser at Rarity's? Dresses and struts around like a model? Ellen Felicity."

Anita nodded. "Sure."

"I saw her yesterday morning, and she was in the last place you'd expect. You'll never guess."

Neither of them offered a guess, and I couldn't wait to get on with my story. "I'll tell you. It was that dirty old alley beside the hardware store. And she was having a row with some big, scruffy-looking man. He was the kind of guy she would never be seen with, so I was afraid she was in trouble. Maybe he'd attacked her and dragged her back there. I thought I was going to have to run in and help her."

Anita gasped and put her hand over her mouth. Clair asked, "What happened?"

"I should have known. The woman was mad but not afraid. When she took charge of the situation, I got out of there, quick. Didn't want her to see me."

A young waitress arrived with a tray holding Clair and Anita's breakfast and a pot of fresh coffee. Anita began helping to unload it. "Thanks Melody. How's school going?"

"It's going great, Mrs. Corbin. Only a few months and I'll be finished. Can't wait until I can get a hairdressing job. Mrs. Peabody said she'd find a place for me at The Rare Curl."

"You'll be a nice addition to the salon."

"Your breakfast will be right up Mrs. Halloren."

Melody returned to the kitchen. "Sweet girl. I hope there's a spot for her when she graduates. I don't suppose I can expect Rarity to give her Ellen Felicity's job." I slapped a hand over my mouth. "Sorry, that wasn't nice. I was going to try to change my attitude toward her."

Anita sipped her coffee. "I wonder who Ellen was with in the alley. There are plenty of scruffy men in town. None of whom I'd connect with her."

"What was she doing? That isn't a place people normally conduct business. At least, not legal business." Clair stirred fruit into her yogurt. "With the outfits she wears, I sure wouldn't walk back there without good reason."

"Is she married?" Anita spoke through a bite of her sandwich.

The question stumped me. "I don't know. Working in the salon, I should know all about her. I sure hear all the details of Stacy and Rarity's lives. Ellen's never mentioned a husband or anything about her private life. Guess I thought she didn't have one."

Clair pointed her spoon at me. "So, what did she say when you asked her why she was in the alley?"

I shook my head and stared at my friend while Melody placed my breakfast on the table. "I didn't ask."

"Why not?"

I held the egg and white cheddar cheese sandwich an inch from my mouth, the aroma causing my stomach to rumble. My friends held my eyes, waiting for an answer. With a sigh, I put my breakfast back on the plate. "The woman intimidates me. She never offers information and doesn't seem to enjoy talking. At least, not to me. I think she might confide in Rarity sometimes, in private."

I managed a bite of my sandwich and swallowed. "I did try to get information in a round-about way. I guess I never came right out and asked her."

Anita giggled. "You are such a noodle. I would have said something like, 'What on earth were you doing in that dirty old alley?' or 'Who was that guy you were with in the shadows? Do you have a boyfriend we don't know about?'"

"No. I don't think I could have asked that. Whenever I have a conversation with Ellen, I leave it feeling like an idiot."

After another bite of sandwich, I thought I'd redeem myself. "I did ask if anything was wrong because she seemed upset. I said something about wondering if she'd been mugged."

Clair and Anita stopped eating to gaze at me.

Clair laughed. "That was dumb."

"And you wonder why I'm not a crime writer. With such interrogation skills. Anyway, I didn't want Ellen to think I was spying on her."

Anita dabbed her chin with a napkin. "Because you were."

"No. I happened to see her. Then, yes, I spied on her. In my defense, at first I thought she was in trouble and might need assistance. But when it was obvious she could take care of herself, I ran.

"Anyway, I had no luck in getting information from her. Ellen had the same reaction as the two of you. 'What's wrong with the feeble-mined receptionist?'"

Chapter Twenty-Three

I walked through a quiet Rare Curl, picking up magazines and coffee cups left out the evening before. Stacy must have had a late night. Neither Stacy nor Rarity was due in until noon, the end of my shift. Ellen had taken the day off, an unusual occurrence for her. Four hours to myself, and all I had to do was answer the phone and browse a fashion magazine. The silence should have been peaceful but a vague foreboding had settled around me.

After leafing through the first magazine, I couldn't bear sitting any longer. I took the coffee pot to the supply room, squirted in dish soap and filled it with hot water. While I ran a dishrag around the inside of the pot, chills tickled my spine. It was the sensation I sometimes experienced when I thought someone might be watching me. Also from my imagination when I'd read too many thrillers. I turned off the water and slowly twisted to glance over my shoulder.

Ellen Felicity stood in the doorway. I jumped and hiccupped a little scream. The coffee pot slid from my hand and clattered into the sink. I grabbed it, turning it carefully to search for cracks or chips.

When I returned my attention to the doorway, Ellen hadn't moved. The chills now ran from my toes to the top of my head.

"Whew. You startled me. With the water running, I didn't hear you come in. It's a good thing I didn't break Rarity's coffee pot."

Ellen remained still. She could outlast me in any silent debate. I wished I hadn't watched a zombie movie the night before, and felt the need to break the trance. "Did you change your mind about taking the day off?" Dumb question. She would never work in the casual clothes she wore.

Ellen continued the icy stare, making me so nervous I couldn't think of anything else to say. So, I resorted to staring back at her.

At last, when she decided to speak, I hardly recognized her voice. She'd lost the accent. "No, I'm not working, but I am here to take care of business." While she'd never been a warm person, this had me feeling as if we'd stepped into a deep freeze.

I forced myself to be nonchalant while praying she'd go away. "Oh. Okay." I turned back to the sink and began to refill the coffee carafe. Feeling her eyes on my back, I couldn't stand it any longer. The pot was only half full, but I jerked it from the sink and pivoted to carry it to the coffee bar.

Ellen stood her ground and blocked the door.

"Excuse me. I'll get the coffee started. Sounds good on a chilly day like today, doesn't it?"

"Put it back on the counter." Her voice echoed flat, reminding me of the zombie queen of the night before.

No more of those movies.

I had more than a tickle in my spine, now. My whole body was sending off electric shocks. "Um, okay. But I should get to the reception desk in case someone needs help."

"That won't be a problem. I locked the door and hung out the closed sign."

Crap.

"That isn't wise, is it? What if someone wants to buy hair spray or make an appointment?"

Ellen lifted her right hand. Light reflected from the blades of her haircutting shears. Very long and very sharp.

She spoke, again, in that creepy zombie voice. "You can tell me right now and we won't have any trouble."

My eyes were riveted on the blades of her shears. "I don't understand. Tell you what?"

"Don't try to kid me. You know what I'm asking. Where did you put the photo album? You've hidden it. I searched every inch of your house and I couldn't find it."

"What photo album? I don't know what you're talking about." I'm not a good liar.

"Now you're making me angry. I know you have the book. You and that friend of yours talked about it right in front of me. I bet you had quite a laugh when you saw my husband's picture. Did you enjoy ridiculing me and Teddy?"

"Teddy? I don't know any Teddy. Yes, we talked about an album, but we didn't laugh at anyone. I would never ridicule you."

"I'm being patient with you. Don't try to bluff me. You knew Teddy was my husband. He was at your house."

If she was exhibiting patience, it seemed to be wearing thin. Her breathing steadily accelerated, and a blush crept from her neck to her cheeks.

I was feeling a bit over-heated, myself.

"He is a kind man, so unsophisticated. It's an attractive quality, and women always take advantage of him. That Utkin woman seduced my man. She got to him in a weak moment, and she took pictures. Then, she demanded our money to keep quiet."

"Your husband was at my house? I don't know who you mean. Didn't even know you were married."

Ellen began breathing even faster, spewing out words. "You keep lying to me! He was there, working on that tree of yours. You probably flirted with him, too. He spent a week working for you, much longer than necessary."

Ellen never moved. How could she breathe so hard and not blink? The crime-fighting women in my favorite novels would think of something clever to say, to deescalate the situation.

"My tree? Oh, you mean Ted the handyman? That Teddy is your husband? I didn't know you two were married. That's nice. He seems like a nice man."

Not particularly clever, and not successful in calming her. After that attempt, I couldn't think of anything other than her cold eyes and the pointy shears in her hand.

"Ha! Now I know you're trying to play me. You knew. That's why you hired him. I kept our marriage a secret, but everybody says you're a detective. I should have known I had to be careful around you."

In a flash of detective brilliance, I thought I'd use

the truth to sway her. "Nope. I didn't know you were married. You're correct, though, I found a photo album. But Ted wasn't in it. At least, I never saw his picture. I just leafed through the photographs. There were so many, and I didn't recognize the men. Except one. And it wasn't Ted. It was another guy in town."

"Give me the book."

"I don't have the book. You know I don't. You searched my house."

"That other woman. Your friend. No wonder I couldn't find it. She has it." Ellen raised her arm with the shears pointed at me. "Call her. Tell her to get over here right away, and to bring the album."

"No. Anita doesn't have the book. We wanted the police to find it so we left it at Valentina's and wrote a note telling them to search the house."

Ellen's scream bounced off the walls in the small room. Her eyes weren't cold anymore. They were flaming. "The police? You gave it to the police? It'll be in the newspaper. Everyone will know."

So much for deescalating the situation.

I pushed the small of my back against the sink. "You didn't hear me correctly. We didn't give it to them. I'm sure it's still in the drawer at Valentina's house. You can go over and get it. I won't say anything. I didn't want the police to know I was there, anyway."

For a moment, my attention was drawn away from the blades in her hand. A strange thing had happened to Ellen's hair. It was all out of place, standing at frizzy angles. Those normally sleek blond tresses grew fluffier and wilder as she ranted. Her cheeks flamed and her eyes were more red than blue.

"Teddy told me about the picture that Utkin

woman took of them together, but he didn't know where it was. Then I heard you talking about the photo album, and I knew. You talked about it right here in the salon, knowing I could hear you. You and that friend of yours were taunting me. You knew all along. Did you enjoy embarrassing me because my husband had an affair?" Ellen advanced toward me, swinging the shears and slicing the air. If the blades had slipped from her hand, I'd have been pinned to the wall.

It was then I became aware of the coffee pot, still clenched in my sweaty hand, so I shoved it at Ellen with as much force as I could muster. She stumbled backwards, struggling to maintain her footing.

The pot crashed, sending splintered glass skittering across the floor. I took the opportunity to push around Ellen and shove her to the wall.

I hustled through the salon and gave the front door a yank, almost dislocating my shoulder because it was locked. As I fumbled, trying to release the bolt lock, I could hear the rat-a-tat-tat of footsteps behind me. She was close, so I gave up on the lock and spun around in time to see the crazed woman lunge at me. I leapt out of her path and vaulted to the back of the reception desk. She came after me, and we danced back and forth around the desk. Every few seconds, Ellen swung the shears at me. With each swing, the blades came within inches of slashing my face. I reached for the phone several times, but Ellen swung the shears before I could lay a hand on it.

In a desperate search of a better offensive plan, I slowed my retreat. As my assailant caught up with me, I waited until she was close enough to shove the desk chair at her. Caught off guard, she stumbled over it.

This gave me a chance to grab the shears from her hand. In perfect choreography, I stuck out my foot. Ellen tripped and tumbled to the floor. I took my chance to straddle her, pinning her down, while I tossed the weapon across the room.

Ellen let out a breath and with it the fight seemed to leave her. She lay still, so I reached for the phone and dialed the Evelynton Police department.

When I replaced the receiver, she lifted her head. "Get off me."

"No."

While we waited for the shrill whine of the sirens, I thought I'd reason with her. "I promise I didn't know your husband's picture was in that book. How would I know you were married? You never talked to me. And you must admit he doesn't seem to be your type."

Ellen's pretend accent suddenly returned. "My husband was always extremely handsome. But after that Utkin woman trapped him, he lost all sense of himself. He let his appearance go. He gained weight. When he lost his job at the phone company, he tried selling cars, but he's not a salesman. Then he tried other employment and discovered a gift for odd jobs. He was so happy, until Valentina started taking our money. Teddy would never be a high-income earner. But he worked hard at anything he could find in order to earn a living. I always knew it was up to me to save us."

"She blackmailed you. You could have reported her to the police."

"The police? And let the whole town know our problems? Never! But because of you, everyone will find out and be gossiping about us."

The conversation had taken a wrong turn, and I

wasn't convinced I could keep Ellen on the floor if she got riled again. "Oh. I see what you mean. There are a lot of gossips in this town. But don't worry about me, I wouldn't tell anyone."

Ellen wasn't listening. Just as well, since I wasn't making much sense. She continued. "I had to re-invent myself so I could earn enough money to save our house. Had to show people I was a better hair stylist than anyone else in town, or in the state. I changed everything—my appearance, personality, my voice, because I knew I could earn enough to pay all our bills. Then we would live in the way we deserved. Soon, I'll have women coming from all over the country for my styling expertise."

"That dream may be over. You might want to set more obtainable goals, now. The police are on the way."

Ellen began to struggle again. "It doesn't have to be over. If you'd let me up and forget what's happened I can still make it."

Her wiggling almost toppled me, so I threw myself over her, spread-eagled to pin her arms and legs. "I'm sorry Ellen. I can't let you go. You killed a woman."

"What? I did not kill Valentina Utkin. Whoever it was did me a favor. They did the whole town a favor. She was a wicked woman and deserved murdering."

Sirens sounded on the street. I uttered a prayer of thanks that help would arrive at any moment.

"It's over Ellen. The authorities are here. There's no way out. Things will go easier for you if you confess."

Guess I shouldn't have said that. She started to push against me again. "Let me go. That woman deserved to die. She took advantage of my man. As if that wasn't enough, she tried to ruin us. We gave her everything to keep her quiet. My poor love drained our savings in order to pay her. All because he didn't want to let me know how he'd failed me. When there was nothing left, he had to tell me the whole story."

I heard a squad car screech to a halt in front of the salon.

"The woman was despicable. I could have murdered her—should have. But I didn't get the opportunity. All I did was tell my Teddy to let her know it was over. There was no more money."

Banging on the door told me the police had arrived. I looked up to see Amos Smith peering through the glass. He pointed at the latch. I shrugged in response, still holding Ellen's arms. It seemed to me he could see that if I got up, she would be free to batter me with whatever happened to be within reach.

Amos continued to tap on the door and indicate I should unlock it.

Crap. With a deep breath, I let go of Ellen and jumped to my feet. I ran to the door. This time the bolt released. When I looked back at Ellen, there was nothing to worry about. She was still on the floor, kicking her feet, and sobbing.

Officer Smith helped her to her feet and pulled handcuffs from his back pocket. She obediently placed her hands behind her back. "Officer, this is a mistake. I didn't do anything wrong."

I planted my fists on my hips. "Yes you did. What do you call trying to stab me with your haircutting shears?"

"That was your fault. All you had to do was give

me the photo album."

Officer Smith glanced from Ellen to me. "What photo album? You ladies were fighting over pictures? The Chief's going to be mad if I came all the way over here to settle a tiff over selfies."

Chapter Twenty-Four

Ellen, hands cuffed behind her back, stood in the center of the salon waiting room, glaring at Officer Smith. Had to admire her for maintaining an air of authority even in that situation. I'd taken refuge in a dryer chair when I thought my legs would no longer hold me.

We all twisted toward the front door when it burst open letting in a gust of cold air and one big scruffy man. Ted the handyman filled the doorway and scanned the room. I scrunched down in my chair to avoid his gaze, which moved from me to the police officer, and finally rested on Ellen. He lumbered forward and engulfed her in his massive arms. She snuggled in close.

Ted kissed the top of her head. "It will be okay, honey. I'm here and I'll take care of everything."

Ellen sputtered something into his chest. I couldn't hear the words, as they were muffled by his shirt.

He said, "I have to take charge of this, sweetie. It's my responsibility."

Ellen tipped her head back. "No muffin. You didn't

do anything wrong. Don't let them pin this on you. You didn't kill that horrible woman."

Officer Smith overcame the shock of Ted's entrance. "Who are you?"

Ellen pivoted and stood between the two men. "This is my husband, Ted Felicity, and he doesn't have anything to do with this. For that matter, neither do I. It's all a mistake."

Ellen stood even straighter than she normally did—possibly because of having hands cuffed behind her back—and glared at Officer Smith. "Go ahead, arrest me. You'll find I had nothing to do with that woman's death. You'll have no proof."

Ted looked on with puppy eyes. "No honey. I can't let you do this. I killed a woman. I'm the one who deserves to be arrested."

Ellen twisted toward him. "Stop it Ted. I know what I'm doing."

Officer Smith glanced at Ted. "Killed what woman? I'm taking your wife in for disorderly conduct, and for threatening Ms. Halloren with a dangerous weapon. I don't know anything about a killing."

Ted gasped. "My wife would never be disorderly. And if she was, it's because she was provoked. She wouldn't be here if not for me. It's my fault. I killed Valentina Utkin. Take the cuffs off my little sweetie. Put them on me." Ted thrust out his huge hands.

Officer Smith stared at the clasped hands and cut his eyes to me. "I don't know what's going on here, but everyone better come with me to the station. You too, Ms. Halloren."

"Me? But…" *Crap That's the last thing I needed.*

Amos pointed to the door. "You go ahead Mr.

Felicity. Get yourself into the squad car. I'm leaving the cuffs on your wife. She's the only one around here who seems violent." He grabbed Ellen's elbow and guided her to the door.

"Officer Smith, I'll leave a note for my boss and lock up the salon. Then I'll drive myself to the station."

"Okay, but don't take too long. You'll need to explain all this. Scissor fight. Photo album. Dead woman? This is a mess."

I promised to hurry, but as soon as the three of them were outside, I marched to the back room to sweep up the broken coffee carafe. When that was done, I combed my hair and sat down at the desk to write a note to Rarity. It was short. "Everything's alright but had to go to the police station to make a statement. Will be back soon. Coffee pot broke. I'll stop at the hardware store to pick up a new one on the way back." I'd wait to see her in person to explain.

Chapter Twenty-Five

Officer Farlow stood at the door of the squad room, ready to direct me to the appropriate chamber. The office was barely large enough to house a desk and two straight-backed chairs. "Sit in the visitor chair and stay in this interview room until we're ready for your statement, Halloren. He left and pulled the door shut. I gaped at the closed door for a moment before taking a seat as he'd indicated. I found myself facing a blank wall behind an empty desk. I got up and moved to the desk chair. I faced the door which was only slightly more interesting than the wall.

Muffled voices vibrated through the wall from the next room. I recognized Ellen's high-pitched tones, a bit screechier than usual, and Ted's low rumbles. I guessed both officers, Smith and Farlow, were involved in questioning them.

With the sound of a closing door and the footsteps passing my room, I figured the officers had left them alone. There was silence next door, except for a few muffled words. I tip-toed out of my cell and pressed my ear to the door next to mine. Hearing nothing, I tried the door-knob. The latch clicked and the door swung open. Ellen and Ted swung their eyes toward me. They sat close together, Ted holding Ellen's cuffed hands.

I slid through the opening, and put a finger to my lips. "Shh." I whispered, "Can I talk to you for a few minutes?"

Ellen glared at me. Ted nodded, so I focused on him.

"You seem like such a gentle man. It's hard to believe you killed Valentina Utkin." I refrained from adding that it would have been easy to believe it of Ellen. "Would you explain it to me?"

Ted hung his head. "It's a long story. It started out innocent when she hired me to do some work around the place. She was real nice to me, but seemed sorta lonely. She worked out of town a lot so didn't know many people. She invited me for lunch one day and I made the mistake of accepting. Then, I don't know how it happened, but suddenly we got involved. I couldn't help it. She loved me, depended on me."

He glanced at Ellen from the corner of his eye, and continued. "She said she wanted to see the city, but didn't have anyone to go with. So, I took her. We had a good time and had our picture taken. Then, I was trapped. Valentina threatened to tell my wife unless I gave her money. First, it was a hundred dollars. Then, it was two. Then, it was more. I had to get into our savings." Ted hung his head.

Raising his eyes to his wife, he continued. "I knew I'd have to come clean, so I went to Ellen. Told her everything." A smile crept onto his face. "Ellen's a wonderful woman. She forgave me."

Ellen whispered. "It wasn't your fault."

"I broke it off with Valentina. Told her I'd already confessed to my wife, and I wasn't paying any more money. Well, then, Valentina threatened to tell the whole town what I did. And she had the picture to prove it. That's another mistake I made—letting her know that Ellen was a proud woman."

Ted took a breath and continued. "Valentina started yelling at me. She said I had no say in the matter. Our relationship would be over when she said it was, and not before. I usually like strong women, but that ticked me off. I yelled right back at her. I've been told I'm scary when I'm mad, 'cause I'm so big. I raised my fist to her. I wouldn't have hit her, but I'm sure she thought I would. It was just a threat. I wanted her to stop saying those things. Guess I really scared her, because she grabbed her chest and staggered a little. Then she sat down on the couch and started gasping for air."

Ted stood up and paced to the door and back. "I figured she was fooling me. Valentina would do that sometimes. She was—what was that called?"

The big man looked to Ellen.

She exaggerated each syllable. "Ma-nip-u-la-tive."

"That's right. She'd act sad or sick, and tell me I was the only one who was nice to her. But she was faking. Fooling me, to get her own way." Ted stared at the floor and stuck his hands in his pockets. "I wasn't going to let her do that to me again, so I walked out. Didn't even shut the door. I knew that would make her mad. I got in my truck and drove away."

He lifted his chin. "I worried, all night, that maybe she wasn't fooling. So, I drove back down that street the next day to check on her and maybe try to talk to her. That's when I saw the door was open, and wondered, had it been that way all night? She never left her door open. I knew something was wrong."

Ted ran his fingers through his hair, and blew out a breath. "So I parked and went up to the house. I was going to ring the doorbell when I saw her sprawled out on the floor. First, I thought she was doing it again. Ma-manipulating. Maybe saw me coming. I sort of jostled her with my foot but saw she wasn't play-acting. She was out cold."

"I'd tried my hand at being an EMT once. Didn't like it. Too many sick people. I got down beside Valentina to start CPR, but it was no use. She was dead." Ted shrugged and seemed strangely relieved. "Gone. I knew she wouldn't hurt my Ellen anymore."

"Did you call emergency services or the police?"

He gave a brisk shake of his head. "No. What could they do? They wouldn't have saved her. I'm not good at lying, so I knew the whole story would have come out, and embarrassed my beautiful wife."

Ted returned to his seat and took Ellen's hands again. "She shouldn't have to suffer for what I did."

Ellen interrupted. "It was my fault Ted didn't phone the police. He called me to ask what he should do. I told him not to touch anything and to get out of that horrible place. I told him to keep quiet about it—forget it ever happened."

"When my friend and I found her she was in the car, in the garage. How did she get there?"

Ellen blew out a sigh and stared at the ceiling.

Ted glanced at his wife, and then turned to me. "It didn't seem right to leave her on the floor. She didn't look natural and her clothes were mussed. I thought I'd put her in bed but I would have had to put her into a nightgown. Sure didn't want to do that.

"Finally, I thought of the SUV. She was real proud of that car. She hadn't had it long, and paid a lot for it. I carried her into the garage and put her in the back so she'd have enough room to be comfortable." Ted nodded and smiled at me. "It was a perfect coffin for her. I thought she needed a flower so I got one from a vase she had on the coffee table, and put it in there with her. She liked flowers. A white rose. Did you know a white rose means silence? That was fitting, don't you think? Valentina couldn't manipulate me anymore."

He smiled at his wife. "I took the rest of the flowers and gave them to Ellen. They were just going to die if I left them."

"Oh Ted." Ellen kicked the table leg.

I glanced her way, thankful she was still cuffed.

Returning my attention to her husband, I asked, "Let me get this straight. You knew Valentina was dead but didn't tell anyone? You just put her in the car and went home as though nothing had happened? Wait. You went on taking care of the lawn?"

"Sure. The grass was still growing. I knew I'd get my regular pay 'cause she had the bank send it. I kept doing my job and sort of forgot about the whole incident. Then, one week the checks stopped showing up, so I quit doing her lawn."

"That would have been when her bank account ran out."

"I guess so."

Ellen sighed and shook her head. "He didn't forget about it, he suppressed it. The memory weighed on him. Just look at him. He's stopped caring about his appearance. Hasn't let me cut his hair in months. He gained weight and he got lazy. He would only take a few maintenance jobs, and took forever to finish them. I had to step in and earn more money to support us."

Ted flashed his adoring puppy-dog eyes at his wife again. "And you were doing great at it, too."

The big man with slumped shoulders glanced toward me. "I'm glad you found Valentina. I don't have to worry about it anymore."

I'd forgotten I was where I shouldn't be until the door flew open. Jimmy Farlow stomped into the room holding a handful of papers. He came to a screeching halt when he saw me. "Halloren, what are you doing in here? I told you to stay in your interview room."

I stared at him, trying to think of something clever to say. "I got bored sitting in that little room all by myself and came over here to kill time."

Farlow glared at me. I gulped. "But I'll go now." I stumbled out of my chair and hustled to the door. "I'll be in my room."

I sat in my little interview box, tapping my foot, and biding my time until Officer Smith poked his head in. "Sorry to keep you waiting Ms. Halloren. If you'll just look over this witness statement and sign it if it's correct. Then, you can go home."

I scanned the document. It was surprisingly accurate. Officer Smith must have been listening when I told him my story. I scribbled my name and thanked the officer. I didn't want to wait another minute to get out of that room and on my way home.

Before I turned the Chrysler's ignition, I called Anita to tell her the mystery had been solved.

Questions and ideas crowded out practical thought on the drive. Was Ted telling the truth? Would the teddy bear of a man really have an affair? Was he protecting Ellen? I knew she could be devious. Did she plan everything—even Ted's confession? The authorities would never be able to pin down a cause of death.

I glanced at a street sign. *Crap.* Once again, I'd driven well past my turn. I had to let go of the investigation and leave it up to the authorities, before I killed somebody.

Chapter Twenty-Six

My house came into view and my foot skidded to the brake. A blue luxury car took up the center of the drive.

Would the day never end?

Still half a block away, but I couldn't attempt a U-turn in the street. I couldn't sit where I was. Ducking down and driving by wouldn't fly. The Chrysler wagon was easy to spot. Too late to avoid a visit with Perry Sizemore. Nothing left to do but park at the curb in front of my little home and act happy to see him.

Mason sat at attention on the steps, defending the front door. Even from the street, I saw his eyes warning the large man to keep his distance.

When Perry saw me walking across the lawn, he pulled himself from the cushy Lincoln seat, and ventured to the walk. Mason's hair stood up on the back of his neck and a low growl reverberated in his throat.

"It's okay, Mason. I'll take care of it now." The cat crouched and swished his tail.

"Hey, Perry. Sorry about the cat. He takes his caretaker responsibilities seriously. Been waiting long?

"Not long. I was hoping you would be home soon. Do you have a moment to talk?"

I did have a moment, but didn't want to give it up. I wanted to go inside and shut the door to the world. But Perry stood in front of me, and if I were to be hospitable, I would talk. "Sure. The weather's great isn't it? Let's sit here on the steps. You don't mind do you?" I wasn't taking hospitality so far as to invite the man inside.

"Uh. No, not at all." Perry grabbed the railing and lowered himself onto the concrete step."

Not my best idea, since his mass filled three-quarters of the space. Not much room left for me. I squeezed as close to the other railing as I could, and tried to appear comfortable.

"What's up?"

"I want to talk to you about Valentina. It's weighed heavy on my conscience, and I needed to come clean. I'll tell you everything."

"That isn't necessary, Perry. I just left the police…"

He wasn't listening. "She and I hit it off from the very beginning. To be honest, we had an affair. How could I resist? She was a beautiful woman and I believed her when she said she loved me."

How could you resist? Let me count the ways. Let's start with remembering you had a wife you'd vowed to be faithful to.

Perry continued. "I was a sucker. She asked for money and I gave her some. Her undying love died pretty quickly after that. It started failing about the time she asked for more—a lot more. I told her I couldn't spare it, and she reminded me of a photo we had taken.

It seemed innocent enough when she asked the waiter to snap a picture. We were all dressed up, and she said she wanted something to remind her of our time in the city.

When I denied her request, she told me what she could do with the picture. It was proof of my infidelity, so I paid. I withdrew the cash from my savings."

Mason leapt from the steps to the ground and took off running across the yard. Following his trajectory, I noticed Anita making her way toward us. Her minivan was parked behind my Chrysler. That was a relief. While I was interested in his story, spending time alone with Perry wasn't my favorite thing.

He grabbed the railing and began to haul himself up. "I'll be going."

"Stay, Perry. Anita already knows the story. We figured it out when we found the picture of you and Valentina in the photo album."

He released the railing and twisted toward me. "You saw my picture? Where is it? Do you have it?"

The urgency in his voice startled me. All I could do was squeeze my lips together and shake my head.

Anita arrived to save me, and used her most compassionate tone. "I'm sorry Perry. We don't have the picture. The authorities know about the album by now, and will probably have it in their possession pretty soon. Lauren sent them an anonymous note telling about it."

Perry put his hands over his face. I flashed a glare at Anita.

Anita shrugged at me and spoke to Perry. "Don't lose heart. The police already have their suspect, so they probably won't even go to look for the album. Or if they do, maybe they'll overlook you."

I wasn't sure how they could miss him. The well-known real estate agent, who was also very large, would stand out among the others. "Or, maybe they'll be nice and not mention it."

Anita squared her shoulders and planted her fists on her hips. "One more thing, Perry."

Her tone caused him to snap his head up.

"Whether the police find your photograph or not, it doesn't matter. You're guilty. Shame on you for breaking your wedding vows. The best thing to do is go right home and confess to your wife. Tell her the whole truth. A marriage is no good without honesty."

My friend, Anita, could be forceful when she wanted to be. Perry pulled himself up from the step, and without meeting her stern gaze, lumbered toward his car. "You're right. I'm going home and figure out how to tell Marlene. I'd rather she hear it from me. Maybe the police won't say anything, but someone might, someday. I won't live a lie, looking over my shoulder, waiting for the truth to come out."

Anita took Perry's place on the step, and we watched him back his car out of the drive.

"I'm so glad this is over. Now, life can get back to normal."

"Don't get too comfortable." Anita gazed at me. "You'll never guess what I saw this morning."

Chapter Twenty-Seven

"Stop. Don't say another word. I don't want to know. I want to go in and take a nap."

I tried to look away but was drawn back. Anita raised her eyebrows and maintained a steady gaze.

"Okay. I give up. What did you see?"

She plunged in. "I drove over to Irma's house, to ask her if the police had searched the mummy house, or if they would. She said they hadn't, yet."

Anita grabbed my arm. "So, get this. I was walking to the car when I noticed someone in Valentina's backyard. And it wasn't a policeman. Some guy walked across the yard from the direction of the sliding door. The one we went in."

I looked Anita in the eye. "Some guy? Could you see who?"

My friend produced a smug smile and nodded. "You'll never guess."

"Spit it out. If you make me guess, I will scream."

"You're no fun. Okay, it was Lance."

I squinted at Anita. "Lance? Who is Lance?"

"You know. Tonya's husband! They live right next door to the mummy house. Remember, we talked to her? I didn't recognize him at first. I've only seen him briefly at church. But he walked from Valentina's, right into Tonya's garage."

"Crap. What was he doing there? Do you suppose he was involved with her, too? What are we going to do with another suspect?"

Anita shrugged. "Our crack police department hasn't followed up on the lead we gave them. They sure haven't secured the scene. People are walking in and out of that house. The evidence will be ruined, if it isn't already gone."

I grabbed the railing and hoisted myself up. "I can't take it anymore. No more waiting for the police. I'll confess to breaking into the house and to sending the anonymous note. The police have to see that book." I pulled my phone from my jeans pocket and punched in numbers.

"Oh, Lauren. You're calling the police?"

"No. I'm not completely crazy. I'm calling Jack. He can go with me to get the album and take it to the authorities. They'll listen to him."

~~

Three hours later, Anita and I sat in my Chrysler in front of the mummy house. When Jack pulled up behind us, I jumped out and went to meet him on the sidewalk.

Anita was half-way out of the passenger seat when I blocked her exit. "Stay in the car. I don't want you to be implicated. You still might have to post bail."

My friend pouted, but climbed back into the car.

I stepped into the grass, poised to direct Jack to the

patio door. I'd brought a screwdriver, and after watching Anita, I was fairly confident of my ability to jimmy the lock.

Jack strode to the front door, so I backtracked, trotting after him. After two seconds of fiddling with the latch, he opened the door. How did he do that? Why hadn't I ever learned that trick?

Once inside, I asserted myself and scooted around Jack to show the way to the bedroom. A strong arm shot out, blocking my path and pushing me behind him.

He whispered. "Didn't you hear that? We aren't alone in here."

Jack reached under his shirt and pulled out a handgun. "Stay put." He crept into the living room.

I followed his advice for about half a second before becoming too creeped-out to stay by myself. I inched up close behind Jack and latched on to his jacket.

We'd made it to the center of the room when a man emerged from the hallway with the photo album in his hand. He jumped at the sight of us, his eyes riveted on Jack's hand gun. The book went flying into the air and he plastered himself against the wall.

"Don't shoot, I'm unarmed."

"Stay there and put your hands up."

The panicked man threw his hands in the air. "I won't give you any trouble. I'm just the neighbor."

Anita poked her head out from behind me. "Lance! What are you doing here?"

I twisted toward her. "The question is, what are *you* doing here? I told you to stay in the car."

She shrugged. "And miss everything? You'd have all the fun."

Jack blew out a sigh. "One of you, call the police."

While we waited for the sound of sirens, I listened to one more confession of an affair with the infamous Valentina Utkin.

"I saw that big guy over here several times—the guy who did the lawn. Only he wasn't cutting the grass when he came. Something didn't jive. I started to think she'd been leading me on, letting me believe I was the only one. It made me mad, so I came over to get the truth out of her."

Lance dropped his hands and slid down the wall to sit on the floor. "I killed her."

Anita gasped. "You did it?"

"Yeah. I lost my temper and came in yelling. She jumped up off the sofa. But then she grabbed her chest, and tumbled to the floor—thunk. I stood there waiting for her to get up. When she didn't move, I didn't know what to do. I tried to revive her, but it was obvious she was gone when she hit the floor. Dead. Looked like her heart just quit. I couldn't save her, so I got out. Nobody needed to know about her and me."

Lance shrugged. "Somebody was bound to find her. I waited, but never heard anything. Nobody even asked about her. It was like she didn't exist, and the whole mess never happened. Weeks went by with nothing happening. I decided I must have had a bad dream. Sometimes dreams can fool you."

A slight smile crept across Lance's face, then vanished. "Guess it wasn't a dream. That real estate woman came in and called the cops. But here's what I didn't understand. They said Valentina was in the garage. How'd she get there?"

Lance banged the back of his head against the wall. "Still, I thought I was out of it until I heard Irma talking to my wife about some crazy letter she got in the mail. It said something about a photo album. Valentina loved taking pictures. I couldn't let that be found—had to get it. I tell you, it was no easy task with the wife right next door. It took me three trips over here, but I found the book." Lance smiled at that little victory.

I wondered if he was thinking clearly.

~~

I could have written the script for what would follow. I'd been through it too many times, and dreaded every minute.

Officer Farlow spoke to Jack first. I sat on the sofa, avoiding the policeman's eye. To distract myself and to keep from fidgeting, I planned a crime novel about the mummy woman. Scenes coursed through my mind as I reviewed the plot. Reviews would be poor. After all, crime novels needed to make sense.

In the midst of visualizing a particularly unbelievable scene, I heard my name. My thoughts wandered back to the surface and I glanced up to an empty room, except for Jack. Lance and the photo album were gone, and so was Jimmy Farlow.

"Where is everyone?"

"Gone. All finished. I sent Anita away. It's time for you to go home, too."

"Home? Don't I have to go downtown to make a statement?"

Jack pulled me from the sofa. "No. It's all taken care of. As a former FBI agent, I still inspire a little fear in the hearts of the local cops. I convinced them you weren't involved. No interview, no statement."

"Oh, that's a relief. You are my hero."

I thought for a moment, sorting through the events

of the day. "But what will happen to Lance? He was the last person to see Valentina alive. And what about Ted and Ellen Felicity? Will the police understand that Ted has a kind heart and he meant to do good? Will he go to jail? I don't think Ted should go to jail, he's learned his lesson. Ellen should have known better, but probably shouldn't get jail time either."

"Whoa. Settle down. You don't have to be in on all that. Go home and let the police and the court system take care of it from here." Jack's voice warmed me as if I'd sipped a cup of hot chocolate.

He tipped his head to stare into my eyes. "Or did you want to explain to Officer Farlow how you sneaked over here under cover of darkness, broke in, and found the photo album? He'd be interested in your reasoning when you replaced it and kept quiet. After that, I'm sure you'd be privy to all sorts of police information."

He stared at me for a beat, letting reality sink in, before he continued. "I can probably catch Farlow."

Jack pivoted and took a slow step toward the door.

I nearly fell over my feet snagging his arm. "No, wait. You're right, I've helped enough. Guess we can trust the authorities to sort out the case."

Chapter Twenty-Eight

I thought about a mid-afternoon nap as I snuggled into my favorite wicker chair, listening to the leaves rustle in the breeze. Anita might have already fallen asleep. She'd been quiet for a while as we waited for Clair to arrive.

Then, Clair stood at the door between the porch and the kitchen. "Hi, you two. Hope you don't mind, but I invited Irma to join us."

"Of course not." I did sorta mind. Our back-porch meetings were usually reserved for the three of us. It was our special time to discuss the details of the week.

"Hello Irma. You're always welcome. Come on in." I leaned back in my wicker chair and stretched my legs out. "We were relaxing, now that the mummy house case is over."

Clair stepped aside to let Irma in. "I wouldn't call it over. I still don't know how long it will be before I can buy the house." She pivoted to go back into the kitchen and called over her shoulder, "I'll get us our wine."

Anita popped up. "Take my chair, Irma. I'll get one from the kitchen. And I think I saw a bag of chips in there."

Irma settled into the big wicker chair. "This is a nice setting. I always wanted a screened in porch but Frank, that's my husband, said it wouldn't look right on the house. Personally, I think he didn't want to put forth the effort to build one."

Clair returned and distributed glasses filled to the brim with red wine. Anita followed her, carrying one of Aunt Ruth's mixing bowls, piled with potato chips. She placed the bowl on the floor within our reach.

Irma slurped her wine and began. "Clair wanted to know what was happening with the mummy woman case. The whole thing was a tangled mess. I don't mind telling you I was surprised when it came out Lance had started an affair with the Utkin woman. It was in the first stages. Not more than a few weeks, when she died."

Clair cut in. "Lance? I missed something."

Irma swung an index finger at Clair. "That would be Tonya's husband. They live beside the mummy woman's house, opposite side from me. Anyway, he didn't know what had been going on with all the other men in her life. So when he saw Ted the handyman visit a few times, and then storm out that day, he got mad. Stomped right in and started shouting about how there seemed to be more going on than yard work. He said her eyes got real big and rolled back in her head. Next thing he knew, she'd flopped flat on the floor. That was all she wrote. Probably massive heart attack. Lance feared Tonya would find out about his extra marital relationship, so he took off out the back door. I sorta understand his position, don't you? He was sorry she died but what could he do about it?"

My friends and I looked at each other and shrugged.

"Course, what he didn't know was he escaped getting the shakedown. If she hadn't died, he would've been financing her lifestyle."

Irma paused to take a couple gulps of wine before continuing. "Well the next day, Ted the handyman, drove by and saw Utkin's front door hung open."

Irma shifted in her chair and pointed at me.

"You know what happened then. Ted Felicity went in and, being the way he is, thought her death was his fault."

Anita shook her head. "Unbelievable. So, Ted picked her up and put her in the car. And then he put a flower in her hand. Sweet gesture, but the man doesn't have all his marbles."

Clair sat up straight. "And Valentina Utkin's body got left in the house. That's outrageous. Three people knew she'd keeled over, and no one stepped up to take the responsibility to inform the authorities. Nobody else even noticed she was missing. How could that have happened in a town this small?"

Irma shrugged. "Strange." After a beat, she continued. "Anyway, they're ruling it a natural death. Heart attack. Lance should have reported it, so he's in trouble. Poor Ted will face a charge for moving the body and for not reporting the death, as will that wife of his."

"What happened to the photo album?" Anita asked.

"Packed away in the evidence locker." Irma laughed. "We call it the closet of no return. Evidence boxes get stored in there and covered up with other stuff. Never to be seen again."

Irma tipped up her glass and downed the last dregs. "Thanks for the libation. I've got to be going. Don't get up. I'll see myself out."

I thought, since she was a guest, I should walk her to the door. Those thoughts fled as I sank further down in my chair. I raised a hand to wave good-bye, and she disappeared into the kitchen.

Anita whispered, "I guess Perry's safe. I'm glad, for Marlene's sake."

I swirled the wine in my glass. "Only in Evelynton would these weird things happen. What do you think…" I stopped at the sound of Irma's voice, echoing from the living room. "Come on in. They're out on the back porch. Right through there, and to the left."

The three of us twisted to gaze into the kitchen.

Anita whispered. "Who'd she invite in?"

Clair set her wine glass on the floor. "Sorry, Lauren. I should have walked out with her and locked the door."

We stared at the kitchen entrance, waiting for the unknown guest to show up.

I strained to recognize the footsteps until two familiar faces peered out from the shadows. Rarity and Wallace smiled at us from the kitchen door. Several possible surprise visitors had crossed my mind while I waited, but those two weren't on the list.

Even more surprising was their attire. Wallace wore a suit. I'd supposed, given his age, he might have owned one, but I had never seen him in it. And Rarity always dressed in work clothes. Never the pretty, pale blue dress she modeled today. Her wayward auburn curls were pulled into a fluffy cluster at the back of her head.

Chair legs scraped the floor as Clair scooted to face the doorway.

Anita stood. "This is nice. All sorts of visitors today. What's up?"

Rarity's eyes crinkled and her cheeks blushed.

Chapter Twenty-Nine

Rarity put up her hands. "You girls stay seated. And Anita, you may want to sit down. I think you're gonna need those chairs, when I tell you the news."

Clair gasped. "Why? What's happened?"

"Don't worry, dear, it's a joyful happening. I won't keep you in suspense." She took a deep breath before declaring at full speed. "Wallace and I are on our way to the church. We're getting married!"

I shrieked, and struggled to get out of my chair, determined to be the first to hug Rarity. The chair tumbled against the screen. And I had to wait behind Anita to give Rarity my blessing.

"I can't believe I didn't know this was happening. How long have you been planning it? How did you keep it a secret?"

"Let me give you the whole story." Rarity glanced at Wallace. "I know you won't mind if I explain things to the girls." He gave her a wink that, I think, signified he trusted her completely.

"Wallace hasn't been himself in the last few weeks.

I've been busy at work or might have noticed sooner that he acted strangely. You noticed, too, didn't you Lauren?"

I gave a nod and held my breath. There still might be bad news.

"A few days ago, I sat him down for a serious talk. We discussed what I'd noticed and what might be causing it. After going through everything I could think of, like whether he was eating properly or getting enough sleep, we figured it out."

Wallace put an arm around Rarity. "I didn't know what was happening. Thought maybe I was dreaming. Then, I was afraid I'd lost my mind."

He pulled Rarity closer. "I wasn't going to talk about it, afraid Rarity might break up with me. Why would she want to stay with a crazy old man?"

Anita couldn't contain herself. "What was wrong? Are you okay?"

Wallace chuckled. "You know Rarity. She wouldn't let up until I told her everything. She made me write out my whole schedule, morning 'til night."

Rarity laughed. "The problem was, he didn't have a schedule."

She turned to gaze into Wallace's eyes. "You weren't crazy. You just made a mistake with your medication and became disoriented. You're fine now."

Rarity clung to Wallace and turned her attention to us. "Meanwhile, I discovered something about myself. It occurred to me how important he is to me. I wouldn't know what to do without this man."

She flapped a hand at us. "I should have accepted his proposal long ago. Did you know Wallace asked me to marry him two years ago?"

Anita shook her head. I stared with my mouth open, still trying to process.

"I turned him down. I'd been independent for so long, marriage didn't seem like something I'd be very good at. But now I can't even imagine life without him. Whatever years we have left, I want to spend it with the love of my life."

Clair had been hanging over my shoulder. "That is so romantic. It makes me want to cry."

Anita nudged me to the side and grabbed Rarity's hands. "I can't believe you're having a wedding today. I never heard anything about it at the church. How did you plan it on such short notice? Is everything arranged?"

"It's all set. Today's the day. There will be a simple ceremony. No fuss. We know so many people, I can't imagine where we'd cut off the guest list. Even with the fellowship hall, the building isn't big enough for the whole town."

Wallace laughed. "You know Rarity. Once she puts her mind to something, it gets done. We stopped at the court house for a license, and now we're heading over to the church."

Rarity continued. "The pastor said he'd perform the ceremony as soon as we got there. Why don't you girls come with us? You can be witnesses. Stacy's going to be my maid-of-honor. She canceled a couple appointments and will meet us in the sanctuary. Jack's on his way to be best-man. Wallace called him first since he's farthest away. With you three, the wedding party is complete. What other arrangements do we need?"

Clair found her voice. "Good-grief, Rarity. You're

amazing."

Rarity laughed. "It's easy when you keep it simple. You girls get in a car and meet us at the church."

Holding hands, the bride and groom seemed to glide into the dining room. I think their feet never touched the floor.

I ran through the kitchen, and caught up with the couple to give them each another hug. "I'm thrilled for you, and sort of speechless. But give me one minute to change clothes. I can't attend your wedding dressed like this." I really did plan to throw away all of my sweats.

"Don't take too long, we'll be waiting." Rarity waved as she and Wallace exited the house.

I found a short navy dress at the back of my closet and pulled it on. Grabbing matching flats, dusty because I hadn't worn them in a year, I ran outside barefoot. The minivan idled in the drive with Anita at the wheel. Clair had claimed the front seat and I climbed into the back to finish pulling on my shoes.

We'd driven about three blocks when Anita slammed on the brakes, throwing Clair and me against our seat belts.

Clair leaned her hand on the dash. "What on earth? Why are we stopping here?"

I pushed myself back into my seat while Anita pulled to the curb.

"I'll be back in a flash." Anita hopped out of the minivan and trotted into the backyard of a nearby house.

Clair and I barely had time to discuss her behavior before Anita pulled the driver side door open. She hefted herself into the driver seat, and handed me of a bouquet of fragrant white flowers tied with a blue ribbon.

"I knew Grace had a wonderful flower garden, most of it still in bloom, so I called her while you were changing and explained the situation. She was so excited to let me collect these for Rarity. It's a good thing she was home, or I would have had to cut them without permission. Flower theft!"

Wallace stood silhouetted in the doorway of the church when the minivan screeched into the parking lot. He disappeared into the sanctuary as the three of us tumbled out and scrambled inside. Anita hustled to the front to present Rarity with the bouquet, and then crowded into the pew beside Clair and me.

We'd settled when the door flew open and Stacy hustled in, pulling off a hair color apron on her way down the aisle, to take her place beside the bride.

It was at that moment I noticed the broad shouldered man in the first pew. Jack stood and stepped forward to join Wallace beside the altar.

Soft background music drifted in as the pastor began the ceremony.

Anita stretched to peer over the top of the piano to see the white haired lady at the keyboard. She whispered, "That's the pastor's mother. I wondered how they could find someone at the last minute."

The ceremony proceeded. I watched it through my tears, so everything was sort of blurry. I remember Jack sneaked a look and a wink at me. I remember Anita passed tissues to Clair, who handed one to me. I tried not to attract attention with my sniffles.

Our little group witnessed the vows of two dear friends, dedicating their lives to one another. The neighbor I'd known since the first day of my return to

Evelynton, and my boss, who'd saved me by giving me a job and by sharing so many bits of wisdom, became man and wife.

∼∼

The handwritten sign, on the door of Ava's Java, read Special Party—Everyone Welcome.

Four tables were shoved together, and we feasted on Ava's chocolate cake and coffee. As news of the marriage spread throughout Evelynton, more tables were pushed into place.

Melvin Stoddard, the police chief, stopped in and slapped Wallace on the back. Officers Farlow and Smith managed to grab slices of cake before Melvin told them they all needed to get back to protecting the town.

Murine Baron slipped in to give Rarity a hug. Her husband, Clive, shook Wallace's hand and helped Murine into a chair beside Stacy, before he left.

Sometime during the celebration, Clair scooted her chair over to make room for a newcomer.

Anita leaned toward me. "Now I understand why Clair's been so interested in kittens and puppies."

"Why?" I took a second look at the man who had claimed Clair's attention, and who had just leaned in to give her a kiss on the cheek. "That's Michael Barry, the veterinarian. They seem chummy."

Anita nodded. "They sure do. He's cute, isn't he?"

"Why haven't we heard about this? They obviously know each other pretty well." I glanced at Anita. "How could Clair have kept it from us?"

She lifted a shoulder. "That sly thing. It's hard to believe she didn't let it slip. But not much surprises me, anymore. After living here all my life, I thought I knew everything about Evelynton, Indiana. But since you've moved home, I've come to believe there are as many secrets in this town as there are closets to hide them."

The End

Want to Help the Author?

Do you love the quirky characters of Evelynton, Indiana? Help others find my books. Tell your friends, and leave a review on Amazon.com and goodreads. Even a short note encourages me and makes it possible for me to keep writing.

Born and raised in northeastern Indiana, Lynne Waite Chapman is a lover and avid reader of mystery and suspense. In September of 2016, she published her first cozy mystery. The debut novel, Heart Strings—first in the Evelynton Murder series—was a 2016 semi-finalist in the American Christian Fiction Writers Association Genesis contest. Her second novel, Heart Beat, published in 2017, continued the adventures of three friends in Evelynton, Indiana. This third volume, Murderous Heart, follows and concludes the series.

Lynne Waite Chapman began her writing career with fifteen years of composing weekly non-fiction content for the BellaOnline.com Hair site, drawing on her thirty plus years as a hairdresser. Retiring the Hair site, she has spent the last fifteen years sharing her faith and penning weekly content for the Christian Living site.

She is a regular contributor of devotions for several print publications,and has written articles for many church bulletins and newsletters. She has also contributed articles to numerous internet publications.

Lynne currently resides in northern Indiana with one West Highland White Terrier.

Visit https://www.lynnechapman.com to get to know Lynne and for information on current and past writing projects. You'll also find more information about the fictional residents of Evelynton, Indiana.

Follow Lynne Waite Chapman on Amazon:

http://www.amazon.com/author/lwchapman
And GoodReads:
https://www.goodreads.com/LynneWaiteChapman
Lynne's home on Facebook is
https://www.facebook.com/LynneWaiteChapmanAuthor/
Follow her on Twitter: @LWChapmanAuthor
And Instagram: https://www.instagram.com/lynnewaite/

MURDEROUS HEART

www.ingramcontent.com/pod-product-compliance
Lightning Source LLC
LaVergne TN
LVHW012015060526
838201LV00061B/4311